Heroes of the Realms

Jonathan Blake

Copyright © 2024 by Jonathan Blake

All rights reserved.

No portion of this book may be reproduced in any form without written permission from the publisher or author, except as permitted by U.S. copyright law.

Contents

1. Prologue — 1
2. Chapter 1 — 6
3. Chapter 2 — 8
4. Chapter 3 — 10
5. Chapter 4 — 12
6. Chapter 5 — 14
7. Chapter 6 — 16
8. Chapter 7 — 19
9. Chapter 8 — 22
10. Chapter 9 — 25
11. Chapter 10 — 28
12. Chapter 11 — 31
13. Chapter 12 — 36
14. Chapter 13 — 40
15. Chapter 14 — 44

16. Chapter 15   46
17. Chapter 16   51
18. Chapter 17   54
19. Chapter 18   57
20. Chapter 19   58
21. Chapter 20   61
22. Chapter 21   65
23. Chapter 22   69
24. Chapter 23   72
25. Chapter 24   75
26. Chapter 25   77
27. Chapter 26   80
28. Chapter 27   83
29. Chapter 28   87
30. Chapter 29   91
31. Chapter 30   94
32. Chapter 31   98
33. Chapter 32   106
34. Chapter 33   110
35. Chapter 34   117
36. Chapter 35   123
37. Chapter 36   125
38. Chapter 37   130

39.	Chapter 38	134
40.	Chapter 39	139
41.	Chapter 40	147
42.	Chapter 41	155
43.	Chapter 42	156
44.	Epilogue	161

Prologue

Father, why do I have to do it?

Lukotico, you are the chosen one, not your brothers. We've talked about this many times. Why do doubts assail you now?

Father, I don't understand. My brother will handle the situation better than I can. I have nothing to offer the Samiz. I keep wondering why I was chosen. There must have been a mistake. I don't deserve to be here. I can't do it, Father.

My child, you are where you're supposed to be. You are not a mistake, but the hope of the Samiz. You will guide them in the task entrusted to you. You'll know how to do it; you've always known. Your mother and I will be watching from here, and you can always count on us when you need us. But we will only answer the call when the situation requires it. Son, you have everything it takes to find the Luminaries and teach them their powers and how to use them.

I'm afraid of failing in the mission. It's been a long time since one of our own was sent to the Samiz. There are too many eyes on me.

You should not fear, but take pride and honor in fulfilling your destiny.

Thank you, Father. I will do it.

I was happy for the words my father had spoken, but I didn't feel as confident as I'd told him. Fear and unease still lingered. I knew my destiny had been marked by the wise, and I had to fulfill it. I was the long-awaited light, but the abundance of doubts and inexperience in dealing with the Samiz troubled me. The next morning, I had to go to the central door to enter their world, but I had several hours to wait, so I decided to go to sleep earlier than planned to avoid overthinking my concerns.

When I woke up the next morning, I saw that my entire family was in my room, waiting for me to wake up and accompany me to the door. Seeing all these close and distant relatives gathered around me, and knowing they had placed their hopes and dreams in me, all the doubts from the previous night vanished. I slowly got up from the rest pod to avoid startling my family. They were delighted that the day had come and embraced me. I could feel my love for them like never before.

We all walked together like a parade towards the central door. I had put on my ceremonial robe, but I had the dressing set in one of the pockets. I passed by the library to grab a book. My family waited at the door while I entered the library, and only my little brother came with me. He was very close to me because when he was born, our parents were busy trying to figure out what had happened to Thomix, so I took care of him. He was curious, intelligent, and somewhat shy, which sometimes hindered him from certain activities. He entered the library with me because, like me, he loved reading what our ancestors had written.

Lukotico, if today is the ceremony, I don't think you have time to read a book, so what are we looking for exactly?

Viktor, I want to be prepared for the journey, and a book always helps. But this time, I'm looking for something I might need during my stay there. I'm not quite sure yet. Check that side, and if you find an interesting book I might need, show it to me.

Perfect.

Initially, I thought about looking in the section on food recipes, but I realized that many ingredients couldn't be found in the Samiz realm. So I went to the medicine section, but I faced the same issue. When I was about to go get Viktor to leave, I saw a book that seemed unattractive from a distance. Still, as I approached, I saw the title: "Ancient Powers of the Antler." I picked it up and went to find Viktor.

Viktor, did you find anything? I picked up a book about the Luminaries.

I found this book.

Viktor showed me the book he had picked up. It seemed a bit old, with deteriorated pages, and its title was "Survival Inventions". I took it with curiosity to see what it contained, and I decided to keep it.

Thanks, Viktor. It looks useful. Let's go; the family is waiting for us.

We left the library and joined our family to continue the journey. Along the way, I saw some who seemed happy to see me, while others appeared upset. However, they all shared the amazement of seeing someone as young as me wearing ceremonial attire. I paid no heed to the criticisms, as I had already criticized myself enough the night before. Upon arriving at the central door's enclosure, we saw 30 wise elders waiting at the entrance and a few others surrounding the door. There were hundreds of people gathered around the enclosure, eagerly awaiting the ceremony. As we approached, my family separated from me, leaving me alone with my brother and parents. The grand sage approached me and spoke:

Lukotico, do you accept the mission on behalf of the Antler people and promise to carry it out to the best of your ability?

I accept, I said.

With the power granted to me by the ancient scriptures and having seen the future, I, Santhiago, name you the Robotic. We hope you can handle this new responsibility. The faith and hopes of our people rest upon you. Do not fail us.

Then, the door opened, revealing a portal leading to a random location in any of the Samiz realms.

May I say goodbye to them before I go?

Of course.

My mother was the first to embrace me, showering me with kisses while crying inconsolably. She said:

We all know your worth, and you are prepared. Be careful in case they don't receive you as warmly as Thomix. Visit us whenever you can. I'll miss you. Call me anytime you want, even if your father doesn't answer, I will, whenever you need.

Thank you; I will.

Next was my father, who, emotional and on the verge of tears, told me:

I want you to know that I'm proud of you, and no matter what you do there, we'll still love you. Be careful, and stay alert. Luther from the Night Whispers may be lurking.

Finally, Viktor, crying, clung to my leg and said:

Lukotico, don't go; don't leave me here alone.

Viktor, you're not alone. All the family members here love and appreciate you. You'll only be alone if you voluntarily isolate yourself, and even then, we'll always be in your heart, supporting you. Today, I have to go, but I want you to know that wherever I go, you'll always have a place in my heart, Viktor. I love you; never forget that.

Viktor seemed satisfied with the words I had said, but he still seemed hesitant to let go of my leg. When he finally released me, I took the opportunity to step back in case he changed his mind. Overwhelmed, I said:

Goodbye, everyone. Thank you for everything. You have illuminated my path, and now it's my turn to illuminate the path for others. Don't forget me, because I won't.

Chapter 1

In a large silvery lake, under the red moon, an imposing and majestic being arose. Even though it was night, the moon illuminated its black body with fluorescent yellow figures running through it, forming a pattern used by the realms for war, as if they were war paintings.

It had an oval dark head with a neck not longer than 3 mouse tails, showing no expression, as it seemed to have no face. Instead, a kind of crystal with hundreds of scattered luminous points crossed its "face." The being was about the height of 3 spinning tops, shorter than an elephant but taller than a lion. It glided across the lake toward them.

The chosen ones had been awakened by the moonlight seconds after the being began to emerge from the depths of the lake. The six emperors had been sleeping there that night, hoping the night whisperers would hear their pleas. They were nervous because calling a whisperer was always a risk, as they held far more power than the emperors, and the power of the realms could be taken away if they became angry.

On the other hand, the Antler people were a peaceful realm with the sole purpose of aiding the Samiz in fulfilling their destiny and ensuring their survival. The last appearance of a robotic being had been three centuries ago in the same location. According to the prophecies of the spiritual leaders, a robotic being was created by the very Antler and came into the world just before a war to seek and find the luminaries who would lead the realms to victory.

The last robotic, Thomix, was ambushed and destroyed shortly after emerging by the Teheritas, fanatics of the night whisperers. After that incident, no more robotic beings appeared, even though their appearance had been fervently requested by every inhabitant of the six realms in the middle of the ten-year Winter War.

That's why the Samiz turned to the night whisperers as a last resort. The night whisperers were a clan composed of Antler exiles who always came when the Samiz called them. The six emperors gathered in formation, tense and alert. When the being was close enough, it spoke to them:

Chapter 2

Hello everyone, I am the one you've been waiting for. I am Luther from the Night Whisperers. It's a pleasure to meet you. I've heard a lot about all of you. I come in peace, and I've come to search for the new Luminaries.

The Emperor of the Horned Realm was the first to address Luther:

Welcome. I am Thorn, Emperor of the Horned Realm. It's a pleasure. Let's hope for a good relationship. These emperors are:

Looking at Flumen, he said:

This is Flumen, Emperor of the Feathered Realm.

Pleased to meet you, Flumen said.

This is Ferro, Emperor of the Horseshoe Realm.

My kingdom and my pegasi are at your disposal, Ferro said.

She is Terra, Empress of the Subterranean Realm.

Anything you need, I am here to serve, Terra said.

She is Coralina, Empress of the Aquatic Realm.

The ocean is yours, Coralina said.

And finally, she is Empress Tecna of the Volcanic Realm.

I hope to learn new things from you, Luther, Tecna said.

Luther stood in front of everyone and said:

As you may know, the Astral Realm is ruled by the Antlers, but there is also the clan of the Night Whisperers. The Antlers are our enemies, so my idea is to find the Luminaries before the Antlers do. That's why I need your help. I will visit the 6 realms and I need access everywhere, as the Luminaries could be anywhere, even where you least expect it. I also want you to look for individuals who stand out from the norm in any way or have any uniqueness that could be an indication of being a Luminary.

In unison, they replied: Your words are orders to our ears, Luther.

Chapter 3

In another part of the kingdom, a portal opened, and Lukotico emerged from it. He was dressed in ceremonial robes and had the appearance of an Antler. Lukotico carried a bag with two books and a dressing set. He felt a bit dizzy from the journey but was happy that it had gone smoothly.

Before anything else, he mentally set some objectives. First, he needed to locate himself; then, he had to find a way to camouflage himself to avoid recognition. Lastly, he had to begin searching for the lumínicos. To do that, he thought it best to find a quiet and solitary place to start reading the book of Ancestral Powers of the Antler.

Lukotico looked around and observed an open area covered with sizable enclosures. He also noticed that the portal had appeared on a hill not very far from civilization, giving him the advantage of observing the attire of the Samiz from that kingdom for his disguise. He saw various Samiz alongside elephants of different kinds, some ready for war, others for carrying, and others for their elegance. It was clear he had arrived in the kingdom of the horns.

After some time of observing the Samiz, he decided it was time to get dressed. Lukotico thought that clothes would only cover him, but his height would give him away. So, after several minutes of contemplation, he decided it would be best to search the inventors' book in case he found a way to shrink his size.

On one of its pages, he found a power to change his appearance without needing any ingredients. He decided to try it, but it didn't work very well due to various factors like not having used his powers for a long time, making them worn and defective. He intended to become an old man, but the power transformed him into a child.

Lukotico put the book back in his bag but realized that when he did, something emitted a sharp, imperceptible cry to the Samiz but loud and clear to him. Lukotico emptied his bag and found his deinonychus at the bottom. He was surprised because carrying astral animals was not allowed. He also liked the idea that he wasn't alone and that, like with his brother, he could have responsibility for someone other than himself. He decided to name him Giorgi. Giorgi was no more than 7 mouse tails long and about 3 mouse tails wide.

Chapter 4

After changing and creating a secret compartment in his clothing so Giorgi would be comfortable, he began his journey towards civilization. He descended from the mound with several leaps and headed quickly towards the first enclosure to find out what that structure hid. Upon arrival, he saw that they were a kind of stables where the Samiz kept their elephants. In front of them were some cabinets where they stored the attire for those large animals. Lukotico was surprised by the voice of a Samiz who asked him:

Child, have you lost your way? the man asked.

Perhaps Lukotico replied.

Where do you wish to go, young one? the man asked again.

I was looking for a place to sleep tonight, and if possible, a job to sustain my stay Lukotico said.

It seems you've found the right person. My wife and I have a tavern with a hostel above it where you can stay as long as you like. I offer you work, my wife can't handle serving so many customers, and I'm busy looking after Trompi, my elephant. The man told him.

Lukotico thought it over but decided it was a good offer and it would give him some independence to search for a Lumínico in the kingdom of the horns during his free time.

I accept. By the way, what is your name, noble sir? Lukotico asked.

My name is Francisco, and yours? Francisco replied.

Lukotico realized his name was too strange to belong in this world, so he quickly thought of a name that could camouflage him.

My name is Lukas, I come from a very distant place Lukotico said thoughtfully, struggling with the lie.

Pleasure to meet you, Lukas. It doesn't matter where you come from as long as you contribute to the kingdom. Come with me; I'll introduce you to my wife, Barbara. The man said happily.

Chapter 5

Lukotico accompanied Francisco through the streets of that city until they reached what seemed to be a tavern. Upon entering, they noticed that a lone woman was serving all the customers at once and appeared stressed as she performed all the tasks simultaneously.

See what I told you, she's overwhelmed, that's why she needs your help. Said Francisco with concern.

Of course. Lukotico replied.

They approached the woman, and Francisco introduced her.

My dear, look who I found in the stable pointing at Lukotico his name is Lukas, and he's looking for a place to sleep and work. I've offered him a job working with you as a waiter.

Of course, if you've approved that contract, I trust you and addressing Lukotico, she said: Hello, dear, I'm Barbara, and it looks like we'll be spending quite a bit of time together. It's a shame we don't have a child for you to have fun and play with, but it's okay; we'll figure out a way to have a good time. You look tired, go get some rest, and when you wake up, come help me clean. Barbara said kindly.

Thank you both for showing such pleasant hospitality. Lukotico said happily.

In the afternoon, after waking up, Lukotico came downstairs to help, and while they worked, he asked:

What is Thorn like?

His father was kinder to the town; we have hope in his son.

Lukotico took note of that.

One question, do people here behave as kindly as you do, or are they a bit unfriendly to strangers?

It depends on who you ask, but yes, people are friendly.

Thank you.

After working, Lukotico went out into the streets to see if he could find any clues about the whereabouts of a Luminary. After walking and talking to many neighbors for 5 hours, he returned as he had come, empty-handed. He went back to the tavern to reread the book to see if he had missed any clues, and he had. Lukotico realized that he had been walking, thinking that a Luminary would suddenly appear, and that wasn't the case.

So, he decided to change his strategy. He would look for the talented and wealthy in the kingdom and interview the most humble and generous people in the realm. He had to search on both ends, but always outside the ordinary, that's where a Luminary would manifest.

Chapter 6

Viktor had his eyes covered with the tsunami of tears that flowed from his eyes when Lukotico, his brother, jumped into the portal. After his departure, Viktor felt lonely in that world, with no one to talk to, share his sorrows, problems, or concerns with. He now had to settle for sharing all his problems with his Orca fish.

Viktor wore a robe that represented his wealth in the kingdom, although nothing he bought could keep the idea that Lukotico was no longer with him out of his mind. His life was very boring to him; his daily routine consisted of waking up at the third sun, going to class until the ninth sun, leaving him little time to enjoy his free time. Viktor was aware that, as an Antler, he was immortal, timeless.

Viktor was envious of his brother for being able to go to a strange and different world for him, experiencing real adventures, breaking the routine, something he loved, even though he had been asking his father if he could accompany his brother to the other world, his father had rejected the request.

That morning, I woke up on the fifth sun, which was a setback because I always tried to sleep in as much as possible, but that morning I overslept. I had been dreaming about crossing the portal to visit and see what that world was like. I was very curious that the Samiz could have the freedom to do nothing, something unthinkable for us.

I woke up from my cryosleep and went to feed Orca. My mother, Tanaria, always asked me why I only wanted one fish and not several. I always replied that Orca was special to me, and I didn't want to divide my love for Orca with other fish. After feeding Orca, I went to the wardrobe, picked up my school uniform, a yellow shirt and a tight yellow jacket with the school logo on it, black pants, and black express boots.

Before getting dressed, I called a domestic robot to bring me breakfast. Then, I put on my clothes, said goodbye to my parents, and left the house. Outside, my best friend Lua was waiting for me, a tall, dark-haired, beautiful, and very intelligent girl. She greeted me as soon as she saw me.

Viktor, come on, we're going to be very late! Lua shouted. Don't worry, it's my turn with Miss Ka, I'm her favorite, and she'll let us into class. I said calmly. I hope so. By the way, I heard about your brother. How are you holding up? Lua asked. Well, it was a huge downer because Lukotico always helped me with everything, but I'm trying to cope as best as I can.

Changing the subject, do you have any plans for this weekend? I asked. My parents and I are going to visit my grandma on Saturday, but we can meet on Sunday. We can go to the restaurant I mentioned the other day. Lua suggested. I'll check with Orca, but I think I can make it. I confirmed. Orca? she said, surprised.

He's my fish. Lately, he's been getting quite jealous if I don't give him enough attention. I said with a playful voice. Lua laughed at the explanation, and they finally arrived at the school, a huge building, blue and white, with a sign that read "Fifth Power School." It was a private school where only people with creative intelligence attended.

In the first hour, I had an ethics class. The teacher, Miss Ka, was very nice, and her classes were very enjoyable. Even though we arrived several minutes late, she didn't punish us like other teachers would have. Ethics was a subject where I always scored the highest, and Lukotico helped me study whenever he could. I sat in my cubicle in the fourth row, and Lua sat in the cubicle next to mine.

The cubicle was a two-square-meter box, completely transparent, equipped with a speaker where the teacher's voice was played, a transparent screen on the wall facing the teacher, and a desk. Each subject had its own customized cubicles.

The next class was on creativity and innovation, taught by Mr. Agut. In that class, Lukotico was always the star student, and I tried to pass as best I could. My creativity was always focused on games, jokes, and unfortunately, Mr. Agut never liked my inventions. I got up from my desk and went to Lua's cubicle to ask her a question.

Lua, what's the next class? I asked. You've been in school for three months, and you still don't know the schedule. It doesn't matter. Afterward, there's the invention design, I suppose you already have the model of your invention ready, don't you? Lua asked. No, I forgot it I said. Again? she said with a tired voice. It's just that with the Lukotico thing, I completely lost my mind. I hope it serves as an excuse. I said as a solution.

Chapter 7

Luther, after giving orders to each leader, went to speak with Flumen, the emperor of the Feather Kingdom.

Flumen, I think I'll start with your kingdom; a breath of fresh air will do me good after the journey, don't you think? Luther asked.

Of course, a pleasure. Affirmed Flumen.

Flumen mounted his griffin, a creature with the head and wings of an eagle but the body of a lion. He encouraged Luther to climb on the front part of the creature, and they quickly ascended toward the winged realm.

Flumen, do all of your kingdom's residents have a griffin? Luther asked.

No, only I and the ministers. The population has birds like eagles or owls; griffins are too precious. Explained Flumen.

Ah, I see. Thanks. Luther thanked.

White gates appeared on the horizon.

We're arriving; those gates are the only way to enter or exit the realm without a flying creature. My castle is to the right; that's where we're headed. Explained Flumen.

As they flew over the houses, Luther noticed that the population's birds had very varied colors and might even be larger than usual. Their houses mostly had the same design and colors: white houses with pink doors and a stable almost larger than the house situated on top, where the birds were fed, groomed, and slept.

Upon glimpsing the palace, Luther was surprised at how dirty it was, with many stains that could be animal excretions.

The palace looks amazing, but what are those stains around it? Luther asked, puzzled.

Lately, there are many troublemakers in the kingdom who collect their birds' droppings and come at night to throw them against the palace. We're trying to find out who's responsible. Flumen said, annoyed.

Still, the beauty of the palace remains intact. I have a question: Why are all the houses white and pink? And what about the red-colored houses? Luther asked.

In my kingdom, we like order. That's why we want each type of person to have a house of a different color, distinguishing the population. White is for exemplary people, yellow is for those who have had some run-ins with the law, and red is for criminals. The color helps us with patrolling. Affirmed Flumen.

How curious. Luther said, surprised by the efficiency.

Flumen and Luther landed at the main gate of the palace. From below, the colossal dimensions of the building could be seen, all in white with pink roofs, and a five-meter-high door welcomed them. At the main entrance, a group of soldiers and servants on both sides of a feathered carpet welcomed Flumen and Luther. The soldiers wore black armor with blue shoulder pads and helmets.

The helmet covered the entire head but had a light blue visor where, in some cases, there was text, graphics...

A servant with a scroll in hand approached Flumen.

Welcome, sir. Here I bring you today's report along with the damage report. Said the servant.

Good, thanks, Sebastian. Let's see what we have today: lunch in the third dining hall and an emergency meeting at eight with the council of ministers. Perfect, Luther, come with me; I'll show you the palace. Invited Flumen.

Perfect, it'll be a pleasure. Affirmed Luther.

Flumen explained that the feathers making up the carpet were from griffin chicks, very exclusive and extremely valuable. After passing the feathered carpet, the palace doors opened slowly. Luther could see several considerable-sized silver lamps hanging from the dome's ceiling in the reception.

The palace consists of two gardens, three dining halls, a reception, where we are now, two kitchens, three dungeons depending on the security level, and thirty bedrooms, plus a living room. Explained Flumen.

Impressive, it seemed smaller from the sky, but only the reception is immense and beautiful. Said Luther, amazed.

Flumen guided him through the entire palace, ending in the dining hall where they were served lunch. After finishing eating, Flumen bid farewell to Luther since he had an emergency meeting and had to attend. Luther insisted on attending the meeting, and Flumen finally agreed.

Chapter 8

Viktor spent the day in the library, where he had time to build his prototype of a nanobot gun with small explosives. This would serve to scare his friends and teachers.

After finishing the prototype, I went to test it with my mother to see if it worked. The gun, when fired, released nanobots at very low power that raced along the floor toward the target. Along the way, they had several small explosives incorporated into their organisms, causing them to explode loudly but being completely harmless. I arrived home; my mother was in the living room reading a book.

Mother, I've finished the scare 2000 prototype. Can I try it on you? It's completely harmless. I asserted. Of course, it's great that you've finished it, but let's test it in the garden. My mother said.

We both went to the garden to try it out; I needed my mother because the gun only allowed firing if the target was human, no animals or objects.

Stand about five meters away. I suggested. Ready, I'm about five meters away. You say it's harmless, right? She asked nervously.

Completely, I'm going to shoot in five, four, three, two, one. I counted.

The gun's shot made almost no noise, but the nanobots came out of the gun and quickly raced toward my mother, releasing bombs that made much more noise.

It didn't turn out as bad as I expected. It lacks a bit of noise when firing, but otherwise, it's good. I confirmed.

I said goodbye to my mother and went to my room. I spent several hours reading and looking at the manual I had written for the weapon to see where it might have failed or needed improvement. Suddenly, a familiar voice startled me. It was Lukotico, but how was it possible? He was in the other world, and if he had returned, my parents would have notified me.

I went in the direction guided by my brother's voice towards a wall with a sheet draped over it. When I removed the sheet, I saw that it was hiding a mirror with silver edges. In the mirror, a face unfamiliar to me appeared, but I recognized the voice.

Lukotico, is that you? I asked. Yes, it's me. I know you don't recognize me with this face, but I couldn't be with my appearance among the Samiz; they would have discovered me. Lukotico said. How are you? I asked. Well, I'm in the kingdom of the horns. A family with an elephant has taken me in, and they're showing me around the city. He explained. Wait, I'll let mother know. I asserted. No, this must remain a secret between you and me. What I'm going to tell you may astonish you, but it's the truth.

Promise not to tell anyone about this? He asked. I promise. I pledged. Good, let's see, where do I start? Well, you know I'm very curious by nature, right? I nodded. So, on a normal day, I was working on the council of sages' archives when I found a document that was abnormal compared to the rest of the documents in that room.

So, before they caught me, I took it and brought it home to read it quietly. I found that the council had an agreement with Luther of neutrality when we both know that the Antler are at war with the Night Whispers. So, I rushed to talk to the great sage, but when I arrived and told him what I had discovered, it made them lock me up for treason, something my parents didn't believe, and they went to try to talk to the great sage.

They made an agreement that I would be exiled to the world of the Samiz with the excuse of looking for the Luminics, but knowing that I wouldn't be able to return home without the Luminics. The farewell ceremony wasn't a ceremony but a supervision to ensure I didn't tell anything to you or anyone and that the exile was carried out according to plan.

Do you understand now why you can't tell parents? You would put them in danger. If the council and the great sage are corrupt, how is it that no one finds out? I asked. They have the entire administration bribed. He affirmed.

Mother knocked on the door, saying that the snack was downstairs, and I replied that I was coming down.

It was mother; I have to go. We'll talk. Can I call you whenever I want? I asked. No, only I can call you. He asserted. Perfect, see you. I'm sorry you're exiled. I said with a sad voice. Don't worry, and don't even think about doing the same as me. I don't want you to be locked up for treason. He tried to console me.

Before answering, I covered the mirror with the sheet and went downstairs for a snack.

Chapter 9

Lukotico went to the stable where Francisco and Barvara were. He found it curious and strange that an adult elephant could be kept as a pet. Upon reaching the stable, he greeted them. Good morning, how are you? How are things? Do you need help? I'm interested in getting to know elephants a bit more; where I come from, we don't have elephants, let alone domesticated ones, Lukotico offered.

Francisco was contemplating, and cutting through the thoughts, Barvara responded. Of course, my Francisco will teach you how to care for elephants; he's the best at it, you'll see, she affirmed. Thank you very much. When do we start? asked Lukotico. Now, if you want, she said. Perfect, affirmed Lukotico. Come, I'll teach you the theory first. Elephants are animals that require a lot of care when handling them.

First, we need to spray them with a bit of cold water to keep them from getting too hot in this almost desert-like climate. Secondly, we need to give them some fruit to allow us to handle them without frightening them. After that, we take the brush and some soap and start brushing their entire bodies. Once finished, we give them another spray of cold water to remove all the soap, and you must give them another piece of fruit to calm their nerves. Have you understood everything? she asked.

Completely, but for riding them, is this process done before or after? asked Lukotico. Always before, so they are clean before leaving home. Although if they return very dirty, we give them a bath only with water to clean them thoroughly, and in the morning, we wash them with soap, explained Francisco. Perfect, thanks, I thanked for the explanation. Now let's try for you to climb up; the first thing to do is to put on the carriage, explained Francisco.

Francisco approached an apple to the elephant's mouth, which energetically ate it. The elephant reacted by lying down on the ground, preparing for Francisco to put on the carriage. Once finished, Francisco invited Lukotico to join him for a ride.Francisco and Lukotico walked through the main streets mounted on the animal.

Lukotico noticed that many more people, if not almost everyone, had an adult or young elephant. People decorated them with different ornaments; for example, those in security had their creatures with lights on the tips of their horns and the rest of the body covered with highly advanced steel armor, all of which were black, including the security officer's armor. He carried an energy charge rifle, very characteristic of security officers from the six kingdoms that shared security attire.

After several hours on the animal, Lukotico saw a man giving a basket of apples to a child dressed in a worn-out outfit, indicating to Lukotico that the child lacked resources for both clothing and food as he seemed very emaciated. After the man handed over the basket, Lukotico saw the child walk away to a shelter where he noticed a group of severely malnourished children.

He distributed the apples to the children without tasting a single one. Mentally, Lukotico promised himself that when he could, he should speak to that child, as he could be a luminary.

Chapter 10

Luther arrived at the meeting where topics such as the search for the Luminaries in the Kingdom of the Quill and in the other realms were discussed. They agreed that the imperial guard would be in charge of seeking and tracking the Luminaries. Luther, on his part, would supervise various patrols, participating in some across different realms.

They specifically ordered to stun the Luminaries and imprison them; they didn't know the extent of their powers and considered them too important to be killed. After the meeting, Luther went down to the dungeons to check if they hadn't accidentally captured any Luminaries.

As he descended, he noticed someone following him down the stairs, cloaked to conceal their identity and unarmed. Nonetheless, Luther swiftly turned, catching the person off guard. He grabbed the individual by the neck, slamming them against the nearest wall, keeping them suspended while asking questions. "Who are you? Identify yourself," Luther demanded.

"I am Fernando, a general of the Teheritian army," the general affirmed. "What do you want?" Luther inquired again. "We've been supporting the Night Whispers for centuries. We've come to assist you. The emperors can only aid you above the law, but we can do so clandestinely. Any task, any mission, assign it to us," the general suggested. "First, I must speak with your leader," Luther demanded.

"Certainly, but there's a problem; our headquarters are not in this realm. Would it bother you if we go to another realm?" the general explained. "No," Luther replied. Fernando guided Luther through the castle corridors to a parking area on the castle's top floor. The parking area had an open door that led directly into the sky. Fernando stood beside the door.

"This is the transport, come aboard," the general invited. "I don't see any transport," Luther said. "To see it, you must believe in it and trust me," the general explained. "Okay," Luther trusted. Bravely, Luther walked toward the exit of the parking lot, thinking the vehicle was there, and fell into the void. Fernando swiped his card over the invisible vehicle, revealing it a locomotive of an old-fashioned train with two aircraft engines on each side. He quickly boarded it and went after Luther.

After several minutes of maneuvers, he caught Luther in midair, dropping him onto the front seat. "Never trust a Samiz," the general laughed. "I see. Cross me once more, and you're dead, I swear," Luther promised. Together they crossed several realms until reaching the Volcanic Realm, where they slowed down and descended to enter through a secret door at the rear of the realm.

Upon landing, a group of mercenary soldiers, all bearing the Teheritian shield, was waiting for them. At the end of the group stood a formally dressed man, indicating he was the Teheritian leader. Both Luther and Fernando got off the vehicle, walking through the group until they reached the leader. "Luther, let me introduce you to the Teheritian Supreme Leader," the general presented the leader. "Thank you for the introduction, general. I'm Héktor, the chief," Hektor said.

Chapter 11

Viktor had arranged to meet Lua to go with the kids to the amphitheater to watch his father's new play: 'Santa is Not Available.' This activity served Viktor as an escape from his problems. He had been listening to his father talking about his play for months and wanted to go see it to confirm what everyone claimed or refute that the play was as good as they said.

Lua was waiting for me at the entrance of my house; before going to the amphitheater, we were going to pick up the rest of the kids. She was loaded with a portable cooler where, as she told me, she had a bit of nectar with liquid honey, a delicious and very exclusive drink because the honey came from a hive that exclusively pollinated the flowers of the Lake of Happiness. She said her mother insisted she bring the drink because the play lasted a couple of suns. First, we went to Álvaro's house.

He was waiting for us at his doorstep, a tall guy with such long helmet-like hair that it was sometimes difficult to see where he was looking. He was one of my best friends. He attended a different class than me because in the tenth grade, we had separated into different classes, and we hadn't coincided in class for two years, but that hadn't stopped our friendship. After picking him up, we went for Pedro, or as I call him, Peter, my best friend, a tall guy with blond hair with brown highlights.

I had met him in the ninth grade, although he had also separated, and now he attended Álvaro's class. Finally, we went for Santi, a tall guy who was in the same class as me, a good guy, a bit shy, deeply in love with a singer whose songs you could hear him singing everywhere.

After the group was complete, we finally went to the amphitheater, which was at the end of the street. It was enormous, almost touching the dome that covered the entire city, a protective security shield, transparent but occasionally tinted with some color so that citizens could see that we remained safe. The amphitheater had cubicles for spectators; we had row two hundred fifty.

The entrance was located at the top, in row three hundred, so thanks to the express boots, we quickly descended to our cubicle, reserved and equipped with enough space for five people. "Do you all see well from here?" I asked. "More or less," Alvaro and Pedro replied. "With this button, the 3D screen of what's happening on stage activates. Look, but first, you need to put on the virtual glasses," I explained.

The five put on the glasses and quickly could see the entire stage, even the actors backstage. "Can everyone see the actors behind the curtain?" Lua asked. "No, only us, privileges of having the play director as a father," I said with a smile. "Thank you very much, this is going to be fun," Santiago replied, and the rest nodded.

The play was about a pack of wolves that had gone several weeks without being able to eat; snow covered their prey, and since they couldn't cover their tracks, they had already suffered some losses due to hunters, as they were easier to detect. The pack arrived at a village, composed of several wooden houses with a chimney located in the center of each.

They went from house to house, asking for any leftover pieces of meat or bones, but no one gave them anything. The pack continued on to the next village, where even before they could enter, there were several hunters with shotguns threatening death if they dared to enter their village.

The pack had no choice but to keep walking, hoping to find some kind soul to feed them or give them a place to sleep as they had been sleepless for several days. After several days of walking, they saw a quite large house in the distance, next to a stable, and they thought that was their lucky day. Upon arrival, they saw through a window a family having dinner.

Suddenly, the youngest wolf cub fell to the ground due to hunger and exhaustion. One of the adults of the pack grabbed it by the scruff of its neck and left it at the entrance of that house, hoping that the humans would see it and feed it out of compassion, and that's what happened. A man with a very voluminous belly and dressed in a full-body red suit opened the door and, upon seeing the wolf cub, felt pity and called his wife, a petite woman also dressed in a red suit.

"Darling, what should we do with him?" asked the man. "Let me see, I think we have some food for him," said the woman. "And what about the rest of the pack?" asked the man. "Check if they have been good, and then you'll know what to do," said the woman happily. The man took out a camera where, upon taking a photo of any being, it told you if they had behaved well or not.

He took a picture of the cub, and the result was that it had been a very good being that year and as such deserved its Christmas gift. The man picked up a handful of snow from the ground, and from his hands emerged a very bright beam of light, momentarily blinding those present. Once it was over, the pack could see how a pork chop with a bone in the middle appeared from his hands.

The woman put the cub on the ground, and the man placed the chop in front of its snout. After several seconds of waiting, the wolf cub reacted and quickly ate the chop. The man introduced himself as Santa Claus, and the woman as Mrs. Claus. The woman started taking pictures of the wolves while the man quickly started making meat pieces for the entire pack. They offered them to sleep in the now-empty stable.

After several weeks, Santa Claus and Mrs. Claus offered them the opportunity to help them in delivering gifts around the world. The pack nodded in agreement. Mrs. Claus spoke to them. "Before that, I want to tell you that to help us, I need to transform you into a slightly more docile animal. Do you accept?" asked the man. The pack coordinated to nod, and the woman offered them some muffins.

"These magical buns will transform you into reindeer, strong animals with a great horned rack," explained the woman. After several minutes where one by one they transformed, the nine reindeer appeared. The wolf cub had a complication; its red wolf nose didn't transform, but it didn't hinder Santa Claus.

Santa Claus showed them his sleigh and arranged them, four on each side and the cub in the middle. With some magical words, the sleigh began to levitate, and the man named each one of them." Thunder, Lightning, Playful, Cupid, Comet, Dasher, Dancer, Prancer, and Rudolph, lead the way!" said the man. The nine reindeer along with the sleigh flew across the sky until they disappeared into the horizon.

Chapter 12

"Lukotico left the elephant in the stable and went to the tavern to ask for something to eat. Upon receiving a couple of plates full of food, he went up to his room, where he let Giorgi out to eat something. Giorgi seemed very nervous when he came out, and Lukotico didn't know why.

After eating, he put Giorgi back and both of them went to sleep. The next morning, Lukotico went down to the tavern to speak with Francisco to ask for permission. He wanted to go talk to that boy. Francisco gave him permission to take the elephant with the condition that he should go slowly, as elephants get nervous with speed. He went to the stable, cleaned and fed the elephant.

Since neither Francisco nor Barbara had named him, he decided to baptize him as Naranjito. When he finished, he climbed on it, and they headed towards the market. It was morning, so there were quite a few people. He got off at a fruit stand and bought several baskets of oranges and bananas. He got back on the elephant and continued on the way. The boy wasn't in the same location as the day before; this time, he had moved.

He was at one of the beds in the inn, feeding one of the children. Lukotico parked the elephant to the side and jumped off. Lukotico had a secret weapon, which was Giorgi. He was capable of sensing the auras of luminescents, so he could easily locate them. Stealthily, carrying the basket of oranges, he approached the boy. At first, it seemed as if the boy was avoiding him, but finally, he turned around.

"Good morning, sir. I'm Gonzalo. Can I help you?" said the young man. Giorgi moved energetically in Lukotico's pocket, signaling that the boy was a luminescent. "The truth is, yes, I'd like to donate this basket to the inn. Could you tell me where to leave it?" asked Lukotico. "Of course, follow me," said the young man. "I'm Lukas, by the way," affirmed Lukotico. "A pleasure, Lukas. In this inn, we survive thanks to donations.

The state hardly gives us anything, and there are more and more hungry children. It's a pity, really," explained the young man. "Forgive me for asking, but how old are you?" asked Lukotico. "Sixteen," affirmed the young man. "Is any of them your brother?" asked Lukotico. "I have a brother named Berto. He's a bit younger than me. Our parents died in the Winter War, so I only have him," explained Gonzalo.

"I'm sorry to hear that," Lukotico offered his condolences to the young man. "Thank you," Gonzalo thanked him. "I want to tell you something, you are a very special kid. Hasn't anyone told you that before?" said Lukotico. "Thank you very much. Occasionally, some mother looking for her lost child, finding them here in the inn, tells me that," recounted Gonzalo. "The truth will be revealed," affirmed Lukotico. Gonzalo pointed to a man with a bag. "There it is." "Thank you very much." "Goodbye." "Goodbye."

Lukotico approached the man and handed him the oranges. He didn't ask any questions, just opened the bag, placed the oranges inside, and closed it again. After leaving the oranges, Lukotico turned around and headed towards Gonzalo."Gonzalo, wait. I have to tell you something. I work in a tavern, so when you need food, come there, and I'll give you food, some cooked, and if you want, I can also teach you to take care of animals. Your brother can come too. What do you think?" invited Lukotico.

"Thank you, we'll do that," the young man thanked."Until then, goodbye."Lukotico left the inn and went towards the elephant when he saw Gonzalo running towards him, holding something in his hands."I think this belongs to him. He seemed as if he were trying to tell me something all the time. What kind of creature is this? I've never seen it," said Gonzalo."Thank you very much for bringing Giorgi to me. He's a very special creature and knows how to find special people. He comes from where I come from. When you come to the tavern, I'll tell you more about him," promised Lukotico.

"Perfect."After saying goodbye, Lukotico got on Naranjito, and they headed back home where Barbara and Francisco were waiting for them. When he got off the elephant, they asked him,"How did it go?" asked Francisco."Fine, he didn't cause any trouble," said Lukotico."My Francisco has taught you well," said Barbara."There's something I wanted to tell you," Lukotico began saying."Yes, anything," responded Barbara.

"There's a boy named Gonzalo, from an inn, without parents, and with a brother named Alberto, feeding many children. I offered them to come to the tavern occasionally to give them some food and help Francisco with the elephant, which, by the way,

I've named Naranjito. Do you both agree to these things?" said Lukotico. "Of course, we always try to help in the village. The fortunate ones must help the less fortunate so that they have the same opportunities as the rest. If at any time you want to adopt them, don't hesitate, we welcome them as our own children," said Francisco. "Thank you for everything, that's what I'll do."

Lukotico went up to his room and placed Giorgi on the bed, asking if Gonzalo was a luminescent. Giorgi nodded, affirming that what he said was true. Lukotico fell asleep more peacefully, knowing that he had finally found the first luminescent. This gave him more strength to continue searching for the rest of them."

Chapter 13

Viktor didn't know what to say, he was amazed, he had loved the play; it was simple but emotive with a technological touch.

I glanced at my friends to see their reactions.

"How was it? Did you like it? I have to admit, even though I like to criticize Dad, it was spectacular," I said. "It was good," Pedro replied, trying to hide his excitement. "I loved it," Lua responded. "Wow," Álvaro replied. "It portrayed Christmas well, I liked it," Santiago said.

As we left the amphitheater, I felt as if I were one of Santa's reindeer, jumping as if I might take off into the air at any moment. My friends seemed to feel the same. We decided to go to a restaurant for a drink before heading home.

Upon arrival, I ordered my usual, a cappuccino with whipped cream and chocolate, a delight. My friends had honeyed nectar. The waiter promptly attended to us, and for starters, we had a serving of chili prawns in a glass, several prawns positioned vertically within the glass, soaked in liquid chili absolutely delicious.

After finishing the appetizer, we accompanied Santiago to his house, the farthest from all of us. The rest of us lived relatively close to each other. After dropping everyone off, Lua walked with me toward my house. She bid me goodbye with a hug, and I closed the door behind me. Mother was in the living room, teaching one of the household robots how to prepare a cheesecake, my favorite dessert. Upon seeing me, she pushed the robot aside and came to kiss me.

"How was the play? Did it meet your expectations?" Mother asked. "It was amazing. It was about a hungry herd that no one wants to help except Santa, who feeds them and turns them into Santa's nine reindeer, with special effects and all. This year Dad has outdone himself, it was fantastic. How about you?" I asked. "Here, teaching the domestic bot how to make your favorite dessert, the cheesecake, but it doesn't learn. It always makes the same mistakes can't put the cake in the oven without yeast and flour. But it insists on doing it repeatedly, and I don't know how to explain it," Mother replied. "Wait, let me handle it."

Addressing the bot, I said, "The cake doesn't go in the oven first. First, the flour, then the yeast. Mix them, and only then do you put it in the oven." The bot repeated what I said in a metallic voice, "First yeast, oven, and then flour." "No, follow the order I told you: flour, yeast, and then the oven. Do you understand?" I said to the robot. "Flour, yeast, and oven." "Good, that's it." "Well, Mother, I'm going up to my room. I'm a bit sleepy." "Goodnight, I love you."

I went up to my room, lay down on the bed, wishing to be like Orca, living peacefully, without problems or obligations. But before I could linger on that thought, the mirror started ringing again.

I hurried to it, pulled aside the sheet, and Lukotico spoke to me excitedly.

"Brother, I have something to tell you. I found the first Luminic; his name is Gonzalo. He's a very generous poor boy who dedicates himself to feeding hungry children at an inn. I'm trying to get close to him so we can go together to another realm to find the next Luminic. By the way, I have to tell you another secret. Do you know who Giorgi is? Well, somehow, he got into the bag I carried and I have him in this world. Thanks to him, I've located it. If you remember from school, you would have studied that astral animals have another sense, the ability to locate Luminics. They have a distinctive aura that we can't detect, but they can." "That's fantastic news. How many Luminics do you need to find?" I asked. "Let me see. The prophecy said the following:

Six chosen ones you must find And a wise leader must show his mind To uncover the great resolution For the terrible and mighty commotion

"So, are there six or seven Luminics?" "I interpret the prophecy as referring to six Luminics and then a wise leader who isn't a Luminic. Together, they must save the Samiz from the bad and dictatorial influence of the Whisperers of the Night." "That might be it. When the time comes, I hope you know who the leader is because I think it'll be harder to locate. Thanks to Giorgi, you'll be able to find the six, but the leader is a different story; mark my words," I affirmed. "Perhaps.

Let's focus on the present first. I must get closer to Gonzalo so that we can go together to the next realm to find the next Luminic. And I must think about what to do with his brother Berto; I have to assign him a role to help his brother but not hinder his task, as if he were his vassal. We'll see. By the way, how's everything there?" Lukotico asked. "Good. Today, I went with Lua and the rest of the gang to see Dad's new play called 'Santa Is Not Available.' I loved it, but I won't tell Dad so that it doesn't get to his head. Well, I'll leave you; I'm very sleepy. We can talk tomorrow if you want. Goodbye," I bid farewell. "Goodbye."

I covered the mirror again, took off all my clothes and boots, and lay back on the bed, feeling exhausted from the play but unable to fall asleep. After several minutes that felt endless, I finally fell asleep on the bed because it was so hot that I didn't want to even cover myself with sheets.

Chapter 14

Luther had finally met the person responsible for the attack on Thomix, who also happened to be the leader of the fanatic sect supporting the Night Whispers, the Teheritas. He had to seize the opportunity and turn them into his puppets, his marionettes in the darkness. Héktor began speaking, 'I'm not sure if the general has told you, but whatever you need, we'll assist you. We're currently scouring the six kingdoms for the Luminaries; we won't take long to find any of them,' offered Hektor.'Well done.

The truth is, I have a task for you as well. In the astral world, there are hundreds and hundreds of my brothers and sisters, and to win the war, I must open a portal. I hope that won't be an inconvenience.'Héktor glanced at his generals, affirming Luther's proposal.'And what do you need to build the portal?''Don't worry about that, I just need a closed-off place and time.''If you want, you can accompany me to the fortress, and I'll show you the empty rooms for you to choose where to build your portal.''That sounds good, let's go there.''Follow me.'Héktor guided Luther to the entrance of the fortress, which had an obsidian door, walls twenty meters high and a meter thick made of granite but reinforced with steel on the inside, making it very difficult, almost impossible, to breach.

The first room he showed me was a large one, unlike the rest of the fortress; it wasn't decorated in a way that would indicate its specific use. The decoration consisted of various rusty and old weapons left on shelves and several books scattered on the floor; it seemed like a storage room for useless items, precisely the kind of room where he could set up the portal.'This room will do, thank you.''Perfect, oh look at the time. It would be a pleasure if you joined us for a meal.''The honor is mine.'Héktor led Luther to the dining hall, where Luther could observe the grand hall, the war room, equipped with the latest in technology.

He was eager to visit the Volcanics, the producers of all technological advancements in the six kingdoms. They arrived at the dining hall, consisting of a large table about thirty meters long and a meter wide, made of oak. Additionally, there were a couple of food bowls in a corner where the pets were fed. After finishing lunch, Luther bid farewell to everyone and headed to his room to clean and prepare it for the construction.

The portal was merely an excuse to easily bring his armies and conquer all the realms swiftly, without their notice, as they were too occupied searching for Luminaries who might not have even been born yet. Nobody knew for sure when the chosen ones would appear, only that they would at some point.'"

Chapter 15

Lukotico lay down after the call with his brother. He found it a bit abrupt how his brother had hung up, but it didn't worry him. He had another problem in mind that his brother, the leader of the chosen ones, had presented to him. Which kingdom would he be from?

After several minutes of reflection, he decided to go to sleep in order to prepare for Gonzalo's visit the next day. He needed to somehow convince him to join him so they could travel together to the next kingdom.

The next morning, Lukotico woke up, went to the well, washed his face, and went back to the tavern to have breakfast: a rat with honey. It made his mouth water. Breakfasts in that era had nothing to do with those in his world. Here, they had a saying: 'Eat breakfast like a king, have lunch like a prince, and dine like a beggar.' In contrast, in his world, it was the opposite light breakfasts, heavy lunches, and somewhat lighter dinners. He greeted Barvara, who was serving breakfast to several customers.

"Good morning, sweetheart. The one coming over there," pointing to the door, "isn't that Gonzalo and his brother?"

"Yes, and here I am, not dressed. I'll be right there in a second."

"Don't worry, I'll keep him entertained enough."

Gonzalo and Berto entered through the door carrying several baskets.

"Good morning, we're Gonzalo and Berto. Lukas told us that whenever we needed food, we should come here. I hope it's not a bother."

"Not at all. Lukas already briefed us; he seemed very happy after meeting you."

"Sorry, I need to use the latrine. Where is it?"

"Second floor, third door on the left."

Gonzalo went up to the second floor, just as Barvara had said. He entered the third door, but the problem was she hadn't specified left or right. Upon opening the door, he was greatly surprised. He saw Lukotico naked in his true body, choosing clothes with his tablet. Gonzalo tried to approach him, but suddenly Lukotico's body completely changed, dressing in his normal clothes. Lukotico slowly turned around, not giving Gonzalo time to leave the room.

From the surprised expression on Gonzalo's face, Lukotico guessed he had seen too much. So, he went to the door and closed it, standing between the door and Gonzalo, preventing his escape.

"I know what you saw surprised you, but don't be afraid. I haven't come to harm you; on the contrary, I need your help."

"I'm sorry, but I can't. You're not from this world! Stay away from me."

"I need your help. I'll tell you everything you want to know, but let me first explain a prophecy from my world."

"Okay, fine."

"The prophecy goes like this:

Six chosen ones you must find, And a wise leader must be aligned, To find the grand solution, To the terrible and mighty agitation.

I come from a world called the astral world. I am an Antler. You must have heard some legends about us."

"I only know that the last one of you who came, I think his name was Thomix or something like that, was killed by the Teheritas when he left. Besides that, I don't know anything else."

"That's true, but the astral world is divided into two factions: the Antlers and the Night Whisperers, those banished from the realm of the Antlers. They live in unadministered population cores, entirely primitive. We, the Antlers, are celestial beings, immortal, and we control the technology of all universes. In each world, whenever a dictatorship or extreme control arises, a group of six beings plus their leader are called upon to fight against this injustice together. The pet I have is an ancestral animal named Giorgi. Any questions so far?"

"But then, for the Whisperers, aren't you the oppressors, and the group of chosen ones must rise against you?"

"Good question, but we don't exile anyone for doing things right, only for crimes for which justice offers the choice of death penalty or exile. The Whisperers are beings who chose exile over death."

"Now I understand, thanks."

"Perfect, so I'll continue. Giorgi has an ability to detect the special ones called 'lumínicos.' The other day when Giorgi approached you, it wasn't out of love or curiosity, but because you are a lumínico, one of the chosen ones."

"Whoa, whoa, whoa, hold on. Are you telling me that I, a guy who can barely afford a meal, have to rise against the dictatorship of the six kingdoms?"

"The dictatorship of the six kingdoms is the least of it, but you've reached the point."

"Is my brother also a lumínico?" Gonzalo asked.

"No, only you."

"And now, how should I act? What should I do? Because I suppose you're the leader of the six, right?"

"No, the Antlers only gather the six chosen ones with their leader, someone separate from us. Regarding what you should do now, it's complicated. Together, we must embark on a journey to the next kingdom to find the next chosen one. There's one in each kingdom. The next kingdom is the Feather Kingdom."

"How am I supposed to leave everything, the inn, and my brother to go with you, someone completely unknown until a few days ago?"

"If you consider it, your brother can accompany us."

"Okay, and how do I know you're not one of the Whisperers?"

"The Whisperers cannot change shape, and their pets reject them. Giorgi respects me."

"Okay, give me a couple of days. I need to talk to my brother, to the innkeeper, and when I come here, if I bring a bag full, it means I'm ready to leave. If it's empty, it means I'm not going with you."

"Perfect, I'll wait here. Do you want to go see the elephants with Francisco?"

"Yes, let's go."

Francisco spent the whole morning teaching Gonzalo and Berto about the uses and care of the elephants. In the afternoon, he took them on an elephant ride through the market streets, occasionally letting them take charge of the elephant.

Chapter 16

Viktor woke up feeling a bit bruised, his head aching considerably. He had been suffering from nightmares for several nights, always the same ones, preventing him from sleeping peacefully and causing him to wake up frightened.

The first nightmare involved him in the body of a family member standing on a pillar in a lake with crocodiles, having to navigate obstacles and jump to the next pillar. Every time he failed the circuit or fell into the water, the family member suffered terrible consequences. Every time he woke up, he called each of the family members who had died in his nightmare to ensure it had only been a bad dream.

The second nightmare placed him in a pitch-black labyrinth, pursued by his living relatives turned into slow-moving zombies. They shouted things that caused Viktor pain. The only ones to assist him were former enemies or criminals, while his own family tormented him. To escape the labyrinth, he had to find a sword to vanquish all his relatives. He woke up horrified at having to kill his entire family to exit the dream.

Upon waking up, I went to the bathroom, washed my face, and headed downstairs for breakfast still not fully dressed, with my chest bare and only in my underwear. I had forgotten to put on pajamas before getting into the cryo-bed the night before, but I didn't mind. There was no one in the kitchen; Mother had left early for the government council of sages, and Father was busy with one of his morning projects. I still couldn't understand why some people liked to wake up early to attend a performance at the amphitheater when they could go in the evening. It was madness.

I finished breakfast, got dressed in my uniform, and like every day, Lua was waiting for me at the door to go to school together. I loved walking together; it was one of the best parts of the day. We had met at the Chamber of Desires, where parents who wanted a child could request one, and she assessed whether the parents would be good or not, then providing them with a child or children accordingly. Our parents had visited the chamber twice.

This morning, I had industrial chemistry and a life orientation class, focusing on long-term thinking rather than short or medium-term goals. Lua wasn't attending my class; she was clear about wanting to become a physicist or mathematician, although we had promised to try to work for the same company.

After the class, Lua was waiting for me at the corner restaurant near the school where we always had lunch. The rest of our group, Álvaro, Pedro, and Santiago, joined us. That day, we decided to order food from the Samiz world, so we had some porridge with bread, which was delicious. After finishing lunch, we said goodbye and headed home. Lua looked at me with a concerned expression.

"Viktor, I'm sorry to ask, but could I come to your place today? My parents are going through a rough time, and I can't study while they're arguing." "Of course, come whenever you want. My home is your second home." "Thank you, I'll go to my place, get the things I need, and then head to your house." "I'll be waiting for you at my place."

When I arrived home, there was nobody there. The council meeting had extended, and Father was still at the amphitheater. I went up to my room and took a shower; I loved feeling the warm water covering my entire body. Suddenly, the door to my room began to knock, accompanied by a voice asking, 'Can I come in?' I quickly covered myself with a towel from the waist down. I left the bathroom without a shirt on and opened the door, thinking it was Mother, but it turned out to be Lua. Upon seeing me without a shirt, she seemed surprised and examined me from top to bottom, mouth agape, and then greeted me.

"Hi, I came to study, but I'll come back at a better time." "It's okay, come in. Did one of the bobs let you in?" "Yes." "I'll put on a shirt." "Whatever you want, it doesn't bother me."

As I went to get my shirt, I accidentally bumped into her, soaking her completely, and my towel fell to the floor.

"I'm sorry, oh wait, don't look down, please."

It was too late; I saw Lua examining every inch of my body again. We looked at each other, and she slowly approached me until our bodies touched. Our thoughts were interrupted when the mirror started ringing.

Chapter 17

Lua found herself alone, unsure of what to do. It had been a while since she last saw Viktor, and she didn't know how to act. She loved that boy his smile and gaze had completely captivated her. However, she wanted to tread carefully; her former boyfriend had hurt her deeply.

She retraced her steps to see if she could find Viktor somewhere. Upon reaching the column, she took the other path she hadn't chosen before and continued until she reached the waterfall. Rather than leaping into the void, she grabbed onto a loose wire. From that height, she observed the moment when Viktor was escorted to his chamber.

Lua was terrified; she needed to somehow rescue him, but there was another issue Viktor's parents were still imprisoned. Lua decided to prioritize rescuing Viktor over his parents; she needed his help to free them. She thought the best approach would be to go incognito to avoid detection. So, after waiting for the kidnappers to leave the area, she released the wire holding her and plunged down the waterfall.

She stayed submerged until she ensured no one saw her. She quickly recalled that Viktor had given her one of his new inventions to change appearance. Thus, she disguised herself as a primitive being with an elk's head.

Upon encountering a group of Light Stalkers, she decided to follow them. When the group noticed her approaching, they asked who she was, and she quickly responded in a way that satisfied them.

Upon reaching the area where all the chambers were located, Lua separated from the group. Using a card she had managed to steal from one of the guards, she went from house to house until she found one with Viktor's name on the sign. This excited Lua greatly, but she didn't expect to find torture instruments rather than Viktor. Fear gripped her as she imagined the tortures and horrors he might have endured.

She continued walking, head bowed, overwhelmed. When she reached a chamber, she read a small sign next to the door on the left the guest room. Without thinking and exhausted from searching, she opened the door, luckily finding Viktor but surrounded by three guards aiming rail guns at him while he knelt.

Without hesitation or inquiry, Lua attacked them, leaving two guards unconscious on the floor and knocking the last one down with his head touching the ground but leaving enough space for him to speak.

"Who are you?" asked the soldier. "I'm Viktor's girlfriend, and I've come to save him. Do you mind?" said Lua. Viktor's face lit up; it was the first time she had referred to their relationship as a girlfriend. "What were you planning to do with Viktor?" Lua continued. "We were going to ask him about the secrets hidden within the Antler's grand dome."

Immediately after, Lua grabbed the soldier's head and released it, saying, "You see, the dome is very weak, with many underground tunnels, like the one we used, that aren't guarded. They are perfect for traversing the city without being detected. Additionally, the dome has no oxygen generation; instead, the Antlers remain alive through microfissures and a single filtration system. Just place an explosive on the only filter, and the entire city will collapse."

Viktor was astonished. He didn't know why Lua was revealing these city secrets to Kaki when suddenly, Lua whispered in his ear, "Your secret will die with you, but your execution will be proof that it will never be revealed again," and she crushed his head with her foot with such force that it crumbled under the pressure."

Chapter 18

Luther began the construction of the portal; he needed various materials, including obsidian glass and uranium. These were not very common materials, but nonetheless, he went to ask Hektor. Hektor denied the existence of such materials in his warehouses and suggested Luther speak with the town's blacksmith to see if he had those materials.

Luther grabbed an imperial falcon, larger than a normal one, and went to the town. He descended in the central market square where he spotted a group of young people with several elephants. He was surprised to see them so far from home but didn't pay them much attention.

The town's blacksmith only had glass, no uranium. He filled the creature's storage compartments with the material and returned to the island. He unloaded the glass and before departing, asked Hektor for the location of the uranium mines in the area. Hektor indicated that there was only one mine left because nobody needed uranium anymore.

Chapter 19

Viktor went to answer the mirror with Lua by his side, so he urged her to kneel so that his brother wouldn't discover her. She complied and knelt, sitting between Viktor's feet. Upon answering the mirror, he could see his brother, but there were two young boys beside him.

"Good afternoon, brother. How are you?" Viktor said.

"Fine, I had therapy today and have been with Lua all afternoon; she's downstairs," replied his brother.

"Phew, thankfully she hasn't discovered the mirror," Viktor said.

"Thankfully," he agreed, winking at Lua while looking down.

"By the way, let me tell you the news. I'm officially speaking to you from the realm of the feather. Here at my sides are the brothers Berto and Gonzalo. Guess which of the two is Gonzalo; they look identical."

At that moment, Lua started to caress my right leg with her cold hand, sending shivers down my spine, causing a reaction under the towel.

"I think it's the one on your left, isn't it?" I asked.

"No, it's the one on the right. See, they are alike," Viktor replied.

"Yes," I confirmed.

Lua continued to move her hand up to my knees and rested her head on my towel-covered lap.

"Brother, I'll leave you as I have a guest waiting," Viktor said.

"Of course, see you later," replied his brother.

I covered the mirror again and leaned down toward Lua, grabbing her by the waist and asking, "Do you think this is a good idea?"

"We've been friends since childhood, we've known each other all our lives, and there's always been a spark between us. Let's not kid ourselves," she replied.

She removed my towel, leaving me completely exposed, and I took off her shirt, revealing her snow-white skin with a black top. I swiftly removed her top; she offered no resistance, allowing me to touch her torso. Her chest was well-developed for her age, and I wasn't lacking either, even though it was my first time.

After several minutes, I laid her down on the bed, taking a few moments to examine her. I lay on top of her, and she held onto my shoulder blades.

After finishing, we lay on the bed, and she asked, panting, "Why didn't you tell me you were meeting with your brother?"

"We've only been seeing each other for a few days; we're still assessing if it's a secure channel for contact," I replied.

"I can help you whenever you want. My mother works in the Ministry of Foreign Intelligence and Espionage," she offered.

"Thank you. I'll ask Lukotico what he thinks of the idea," I said.

After changing, Lua said goodbye. Her hair was completely disheveled, yet she remained beautiful.

Mother still hadn't arrived. I didn't know what could have happened in the meeting to keep her at the office for so long. Father hadn't arrived either, so I picked up a book to read until my parents returned. I was starting to worry; they usually arrived late, but not this late.

Chapter 20

Lukotico entered an inn to request two rooms to sleep. The owner, Lola, very friendly, invited them, being newcomers to the inn, to a good plate of porridge with pieces of leek and tomato on top. After finishing, the three agreed to start the search for the second luminary. They were going to split up to cover more ground.

Lukotico began at the palace of a noble while Gonzalo started at the inns and lodges, and Berto at the market streets. Any indication of a chosen one had to be reported to Lukotico so that he could identify whether it was indeed a chosen one or a fraud.

Lukotico entered the palace posing as a bread delivery person, approaching each servant, letting Giorgi sniff them all. Unfortunately, while trying to leave the palace, the palace guard stopped him, asking for identification. Seeing he wasn't a servant, they locked him up in the dungeons. Lukotico took on his original form to attempt breaking the bars and escape.

Fortunately, a noble from the castle took a stroll through and spotted him in the dungeons. Almost immediately, Giorgi leaped out of the pocket and went straight to the noble, ending up receiving caresses from her. The noble, upon seeing Lukotico, whom he hadn't had time to transform, was frightened and amazed. Almost instantly, Lukotico emerged from the cage and covered her mouth so she wouldn't scream.

Who are you?

Before, I want to ask you, whom do you serve, the Antlers or the Whisperers?

The Antlers.

Well, I am Lukotico, of the Antlers. This creature is Giorgi, my pet, and who are you?

I am Mafalda, a noble of the Trigueiros lineage.

A pleasure. Do you know the legend of the chosen ones?

Yes, six chosen ones must fight against the dictatorship, I wish they would come now.

I must give you news; I am an Antler. I seek and gather the Antlers to fight together, and my pet is an astral animal capable of identifying the chosen ones. And by where Giorgi is now, you are a chosen one.

I can't believe it. Throughout my life, nothing like this has ever happened to me, something as serious as being chosen. This is not something to joke about. Show me some proof to know that you are an Antler.

Giorgi isn't enough? Have you ever seen a creature like him?

You could have stolen it.

Let me see. This might convince you.

Lukotico transformed into a Velociraptor, Giorgi increased in size, then quickly turned into a griffin and returned to its original form.

Does this suffice?

It does, but I need to speak with my family. I can't leave them alone.

Alright.

Lukotico and Mafalda parted ways. Lukotico escaped the prison, passing through the wall as if there were no barrier. He went to find Gonzalo and Berto. Gonzalo was in an inn helping the people there with cleaning tasks, so Lukotico approached him.

Gonzalo, I found her. She's a noble named Mafalda.

Mafalda? The noble everyone talks about because she spends more time among the poor than among the rich?

I suppose that's her.

Well done. Did she want to come with us?

She says she must first speak with her family; she can't leave them stranded, but I think she agreed.

That's good. Oh, we almost forgot, we have to find Berto. I last saw him at the market buying some fruits and vegetables.

Let's go there.

Gonzalo bid farewell to the people he had helped, and they left the inn together. They had left the elephants in a stable they had rented near the inn where they had stayed.

After several minutes of walking through the streets, they saw Berto. He was carrying several bags and walking toward the stable. Both reached him just as he was about to open the stable door.

Good morning, brother. Lukotico has found her; her name is Mafalda. She's a noble who cares more for the less fortunate than for herself.

Where is she now?

She went to see her family to inform them.

Okay, I was about to feed Charo and Avelino. Then I saw there was a pet shop in the market; I was going to check it out, we may not have money, but it's worth seeing what's there in this kingdom.

Wait a moment, I think I can help you, let me check my book for a second. Said Lukotico

Lukotico pulled out a large book from his attire titled Ancestral Powers of the Antlers. He searched through the pages until he found one titled: Samiz Money. Lukotico recited the spell, and from his hands began to flow coins and coins of gold. To stop the spell, Lukotico closed his hands.

I think this should be enough, right?

With this, we can buy ourselves a palace if we want. Replied Berto.

We have to be inconspicuous.

Right. Said Gonzalo.

The three fed the elephants and together went to the market to the pet shop, where they saw that all the creatures were flying, making them different and special compared to other kingdoms.

The store was right next to the chicken slaughterhouse; that was the only meat that could be consumed in the kingdom of feathers. Upon arriving at the store, a very friendly man named Delma attended to them, guiding them through the entire store, showing them each animal and their uses.

Then he asked how special they wanted their animal, and they mentioned that money was no problem. So, Delma took them to the back of the store and introduced them to the Sinomacrops.

Lukotico found it a unique and beautiful creature and bought it for a quite high price, five gold coins and three silver coins.

Chapter 21

Viktor went to bed without his parents having arrived home yet; he was very worried and confused. He wanted things to go back to how they were before with Lua, in a friend-like state. He didn't want any more worries.

The next morning, I woke up to some knocks on the front door. Three security officers stood there.

"Good morning, what brings you to this house?" I asked.

"Do Halfonso and Kerry live here?" one of the officers inquired.

"Yes, they are my parents. What's wrong?" I responded.

"Yesterday afternoon, both of them were arrested for rebel conspiracy and treason against the revolutionary process."

"My parents?"

"That's correct. Although they later escaped from prison. We came to warn you; they are dangerous. If you see them, let us know."

"Of course, my hand is fully committed to the Antler empire." I tapped my hand lightly on my chest.

"Amen!" the officers exclaimed.

I closed the door, finding it hard to believe. My parents were traitors to the country. Lukotico's story was starting to make sense, and I knew I was being watched now. So, when I heard some knocks on my window, I quickly opened it and found Lua, whom I let in.

"Hi there, what are you doing here?" I asked.

"I came to see if you wanted to go out with me for something to drink, but I saw the security people leaving your house, so I climbed up to your window," Lua replied.

"My parents are arrested for conspiring against the empire."

"And is it true?"

"It's more complicated than that."

"Do you trust me?"

"I trust you so much that I would give my life if it were for a greater good."

"Then tell me. I won't judge you; you know that."

"In one of the calls, my brother confessed that he hadn't left in search of the chosen ones; instead, the wise ones had exiled him. Under the pretext of the chosen ones, they ousted him from the hierarchy. Now, my parents are going through the same thing, and I don't think they'll be exiled. It would raise too many questions that the wise ones wouldn't answer. I know they're watching the house, watching me in case I'm also an accomplice."

"I'll support you in whatever you need. My family isn't treated well either. As you know, my parents own the national newspaper, where they criticize and praise people for their deeds, and they've been criticizing the government for a while. The government is threatening them. My family is afraid, just like me."

"Don't worry; we'll fix this. We need to gather all the people who disagree with the government, and together, we'll go after them.

But right now, we need to think about what to do with my parents. They're imprisoned pending trial. I know they said they escaped yesterday, but it's probably a police tactic to catch us off guard, so they won't expect us to go see them."

"Good idea. And how are we going to do it?"

"Thanks for asking. We'll wait until nightfall, put on the suits I've been making since Lukotico warned me about the wise ones, and we'll raid the prison."

Lua looked at me with a suggestive look.

"We can do other things while we're at it," Lua said with a mischievous expression.

"We need to focus on the plan," I said seriously, not wanting to end up like the other day.

"I'm focused, but are you?" she replied, removing the top part of her outfit.

I began to warm up at the sight of her. It had to be acknowledged that she had a very attractive body, defined by gentle curves and noticeable breasts that seemed smaller under the clothing. Her expression said it all; her eyes were fixed on my pants, and I tried to resist because I didn't want to ruin the plan for mere caresses.

"Let's see if this gets you more enthusiastic," Lua said as she put her hand in my pocket, stroking my leg.

"I can't do this; we don't have time," I said, trying to control myself to avoid arousal.

"Don't play hard to get; I know you like me," she said, putting her other hand in the other pocket.

"Please, of course, I like you, but I don't think it's the right time," I said, closing my legs to prevent her hands from descending further down my legs.

"Don't think I'll give up so easily," she said with a playful smile.

Lua began kissing my mouth passionately. Her full lips collided with mine; she nibbled on my lips, releasing her passion onto mine, and I eventually let myself go.

I began kissing her neck; she leaned back, allowing me to kiss her. Lua, on her part, removed the top part of my outfit, exposing my chest and back. I never exercised much, but I still had a slim yet defined body. She grabbed my shoulder blades, and before I knew it, she had removed her pants and was trying to remove mine, and I helped her.

After we finished, we were both exhausted, but I looked out the window; it was starting to get dark, and we only had thirty minutes left before we started our infiltration.

Ten minutes before leaving the house, we were both recovered, and together we helped each other put on the suits. Her hips were accentuated by the outfit, and my chest stood out. I had made the pants narrow, thinking that if we were to go through water, it would be better if they were almost like neoprene.

Chapter 22

Lukotico, Gonzalo, and Berto had already been three days at the inn, waiting for Mafalda's response, whom they hadn't seen since Lukotico escaped from prison. Meanwhile, they had been learning about the incredible abilities of Sinomacrops. The creature had not left Lukotico's back since they freed it from the cage where it was kept.

Gradually, they taught it to grab objects and elevate them without letting go while in the air.

One day, it attempted to lift Lukotico, but he was too heavy, and it could only raise him a few centimeters off the ground. Berto and Gonzalo were left amazed at the scene.

They had been waiting for Mafalda for a week, and she still hadn't shown up. Impatient, Lukotico decided to return to the palace, heading straight to the dungeon and waiting for her there. After sharing his plan with the brothers, they offered to help, but Lukotico refused, saying they couldn't change shape, and they were too important to take on that task.

Leaving the inn, Lukotico retraced the path he had taken days before, but this time, he used his powers to change his appearance and go unnoticed. He walked through the market streets until he reached a path marked by perfectly placed and polished red stones, resembling a carpet, leading to the palace gates. Upon arrival, he beheld an impressive mostly white castle.

Lukotico decided to enter by camouflaging himself as a general. He transformed into a handsome, fair-skinned general named Nachojarito, wearing the same uniform as the guards but with a couple of stars and flags to indicate a high rank and prevent any questioning.

At the gate, the guards saluted him and without a single question, let him pass into the castle. Seeing how easily he had entered, Lukotico changed his original plan. He would wander the palace in his general guise, making it easier to find Mafalda.

And so he did. After several minutes walking through the long, towering castle corridors, he spotted Mafalda. She was signing papers with the court seal, looking very sad, almost on the verge of tears. He approached her.

"General," she said, raising her right hand to salute.

"Greetings, Mafalda," Lukotico replied, maintaining his character in case there was someone else in the room.

"What's the matter?" Lukotico continued.

"His Majesty has just stripped me of my noble title, dismissing me for the first time," she replied.

"Let's go somewhere private," Lukotico said. He knew that keeping up the act wasn't part of the plan; he wanted to end this conversation quickly.

"Sure, come with me," Mafalda replied, exhausted.

Together, they went to a room filled with books of all categories and genres; that must have been the library, Lukotico thought.

Mafalda was tired. She had just been expelled from the palace and didn't feel like talking to anyone. She now had to figure out what to do from that moment on; her life had drastically changed. For a moment, she considered joining Lukotico on his expedition, wondering if Lukotico was still waiting for her answer or if he had already left the kingdom. She quickly dismissed the idea; she had a family there. She couldn't just leave without making arrangements in her absence.

Seeing that the room was empty and the door closed, Lukotico transformed.

"Lukotico!" Mafalda exclaimed, surprised.

"What do you think? We're all waiting for you," Lukotico replied amiably, yet ironically.

"You know I can't," she told him.

"What ties you to this kingdom?" Lukotico asked.

"Uh, my family, for example," Mafalda replied hesitantly.

"I can easily take care of that," Lukotico assured her.

"How?" she asked.

"I'll pay someone to take care of your family," Lukotico proudly replied.

"It's too expensive," she said, concerned.

"Don't worry about the money," Lukotico said, noticing her worry.

Relieved, Mafalda finally accepted his request, and they left the castle together. To exit discreetly, Lukotico transformed back into the general.

Chapter 23

Viktor and Lua finally set off towards the prison. Viktor had a secret door in his room that led to the city's tunnels. To access it, they had to move aside the round rug located in the center of the room. Upon removing it, they found a round hole a meter wide with no visible end, it was too dark to see.

Lua bravely jumped in first, without any fear, and without warning, she leaped while shouting with joy. After hearing Lua for fifteen seconds, Viktor gathered the courage and followed suit, though he didn't shout anything.

Upon reaching the bottom, I realized we were floating on water, and Lua was beside me.

"Shall we go down?" she asked.

"I don't know, it doesn't seem very safe," I replied.

"You made these suits for a reason, to dive, right?"

"True, but I'm also a bit scared."

"Don't worry, silly. We'll go together; nothing can happen."

"Okay."

We both submerged, starting to descend deeper and deeper until my hands began to numb from exhaustion and the coldness of the water.

When I realized I had drifted too far from Lua, a column forced me to veer left, separating me even more until suddenly I noticed I couldn't see her anymore. At first, I wasn't worried because the tunnel was straight, so she must have gone faster than me. After several minutes following the current, I started to get nervous as I couldn't see the end of the tunnel.

Unexpectedly, the tunnel opened into a waterfall, at the bottom of which awaited some unsettling beings. Suddenly and without warning, I plummeted through the current over the waterfall. It propelled me in such a way that I remained floating for several seconds, which gave me time to glance at the bottom where there were huts made from recycled metals, I suspected. By their shape and location, I feared the worst - they were the Lurkers of Light, comprised of several tribes living in the deepest part of the planet, rumored to be cannibals.

As I landed at the bottom, I tried to swim away from them, but it was futile. Homemade fishing nets trapped me, making it impossible for me to escape.

"Stop moving, kid," said a voice.

"It's useless, you won't be able to escape," said another voice.

"We won't hurt you, we just want to help you."

Finally, I stopped moving, tired. It was pointless trying to free myself from the nets.

As I got out of the water, I saw three men, all dressed in primitive robes and wearing animal skulls on their heads. The man closest to me introduced himself.

"Hello, I'm Kaki, leader of the Lurkers of Light tribes. And who are you?"

"Hello, I'm Viktor. Are you going to kill me?"

"Welcome, Viktor. We're not going to kill you. I know on the surface you think of us as primitive cannibals, and to some extent, it's true."

I was speechless, not knowing what to say. Kaki continued his speech.

"We are worse than what is said about us. From now on, you're our guest, Viktor, brother of Lukotico, banished with the Samiz. My companion Chiro will escort you to the room that will be your home until we get tired of you and kill you. What do you think?"

Without giving me time to speak, Chiro, who had a deer skull on his head, gestured for me to follow him.

He took me to the third hut, which was quite modern inside, although it still didn't compare to the houses on the surface. Inside, each hut had a central living area branching off into several rooms: a bedroom, a lavatory, and a table for work or reading. The entire space was metallic white. Upon entering, he closed the door behind me, which seemed to only be unlockable with a security code or a card.

Chapter 24

As they left the castle, Berto and Gonzalo were waiting for them along with all their animals. Lukotico was still incognito as the general, so no one recognized him, but Mafalda did. She approached them.

"Good afternoon, Mafalda. Have you finally decided to come?" asked Berto.

"It seems so. I came with Lukotico, but I don't know where he's disappeared to right now."

"He must be transforming," Gonzalo speculated.

"Could be," Mafalda agreed.

"I'm sorry, we haven't introduced ourselves yet. I'm Berto, and this here is my brother Gonzalo. We're from the Horn Kingdom."

"Interesting. What are your future plans?" inquired Mafalda.

"Has Lukotico mentioned the prophecy to you?" asked Berto.

"He's mentioned something about us being the chosen ones or something like that, but I still don't know what purpose it serves," replied Mafalda.

"According to Lukotico, we must go to each of the kingdoms to find the rest of the chosen ones," explained Gonzalo.

At that moment, Lukotico approached them.

"Welcome to the family, Mafalda. Have they introduced themselves?" he asked.

"Yes, thank you. I just wanted to say that I'll accompany you, but I have one condition: that I can bring my pet, Ala Bateada, and her two young offspring. She's like a daughter to me," requested Mafalda.

"Of course, everyone here has their own pet," confirmed Lukotico.

"Perfect, I'll call her then."

At that moment, Mafalda emitted a long, sharp whistle, and several seconds later, three golden griffins appeared in the sky, landing beside them. The largest one, presumably Ala Bateada, lowered her head toward Mafalda's.

"Alright, let's get going then," said Mafalda.

"Okay," the three of them replied in unison.

They all began their journey toward the nearest taxi to go to the Horseshoe Kingdom.

Upon arrival, they received instructions from the driver and all got into the taxi. After several hours of travel, they finally reached the Horseshoe Kingdom. The landscape was spectacular and exotic at the same time. The entire kingdom consisted of a vast plain and a small area of not-so-dense forest. In the plain, several horses could be seen grazing and moving around.

In the distance, the Emperor Ferro's palace could be glimpsed. A large, cheerful, green tower stood tall where several guards were stationed."

Chapter 25

Luther, upon finishing the portal, called one of the guards.

Come here for a moment, I need to show you how this works.

Yes, sir.

As the guard approached the portal to examine it, Luther delivered an extremely strong kick to the guard's hip, causing him to lose balance and fall towards the portal, with the misfortune of only his head going through it. The portal began emitting a loud sound and illuminated in green, creating a sort of quantum door to another place.

The guard remained unconscious at the entrance of the portal, and when the portal finished emitting sound, it signaled Luther that the portal was working, and he only had to wait a couple of seconds. Several soldiers came out of the portal, their leader, wearing different armor, carrying the guard's head as if it were a trophy.

Good job, Luther.

Thank you, General.

Once they finish coming out, gather them all in the main hall, and we'll give instructions on how to proceed.

Understood, General.

After the general, soldier after soldier started coming out, reaching the overwhelming number of 300,000 soldiers, along with all the artillery machines they brought with them. The officers gathered in the main hall while the soldiers lined up at the outer gate. In the main hall, officers, captains, and generals assembled.

It was the general who spoke first.

Esteemed officers, we must be relentless in our pursuit of them and not rest until they have been completely eliminated. Only then can we focus our efforts on the Antler and put an end to this war once and for all. It won't be easy. The Luminics are powerful and well-organized. But I trust that with your courage, skills, and dedication, we can prevail over them. Together, we can ensure that our world is a safe place for all of us and for future generations.

In summary, I ask that you be prepared to face any challenge that arises on the path to victory. I ask that you fight with honor and never lose sight of our ultimate goal: to end the Antler and protect our world. I am confident that together, we will achieve it. Forward, officers! For victory!

After the speech, the generals and officers headed to the outer gate, where they met with their squads awaiting the speech that the Emperor of the Night Whisperers was about to give to the soldiers. Luther spoke with Hektor to explain that now they had an army, they could crush the insurgents, including the Emperors, their supposed allies. Their conversation was interrupted when the Emperor began to speak.

Esteemed soldiers, I speak to you today with the urgency and passion of a warrior who is willing to do whatever it takes to protect his people and his home. We face a double threat and must act swiftly and decisively if we are to succeed.

On the one hand, there are the Luminics. These arrogant and powerful beings have shown their true nature: they are not friends of humanity but see us as mere toys, puppets for their whims. They have shown their willingness to destabilize our society, sow discord, and chaos. We cannot allow them to continue with their machinations. We must find them and eliminate them before they can do more harm.

But they are not the only enemies we face. Behind the Luminics is the Antler, the force gathering and leading them. The Antler is the true enemy we must fight. It is the brain behind everything, seeking to destroy our civilization and subjugate us to its will.

So I ask you, soldiers, to join me in this fight. We must seek out the Luminics and find the Antler. We must do whatever it takes to defeat them, without hesitation or surrender. There is no time for doubt or indecision. We must be brave, strong, and decisive.

It is time to show our true strength as soldiers. It is time to rise and fight for what is just and right. I have always known that I can rely on you, that you are the best and bravest soldiers our nation has. Now is the time to prove it. So go ahead, soldiers. Move forward in the fight against the Luminics and the Antler. Move forward in the fight for our freedom and survival. Together, we can and will prevail. For victory!

Chapter 26

Lua was alone, unsure of what to do. She had not seen Viktor for a while and didn't know how to act. She loved that boy; his smile and gaze had completely enamored her. However, she wanted to be careful. Her previous boyfriend had caused her a lot of pain.

She retraced her steps to see if she could find Viktor somewhere. Upon reaching the column, she took the other path she had not chosen before. She followed the path until she reached the waterfall. Instead of plunging into the void, she held onto a loose wire. From the height, she could observe the moment when Viktor was escorted to his dwelling.

Lua was terrified. She needed to rescue him somehow, but she also had another problem: Viktor's parents were still prisoners. Lua chose to prioritize Viktor's rescue over that of his parents; she needed his help to save them. Lua thought it best to go incognito to avoid detection.

So, after waiting for the kidnappers to leave the area, she released the wire holding her and plunged down the waterfall. As she fell, she stayed submerged until she made sure no one saw her. She quickly remembered that Viktor had given her one of his new inventions to change appearances. Thus, she disguised herself as a primitive being, resembling a moose-headed creature.

When she saw a group of Light Stalkers, she decided to follow them. When the group saw her approaching, they asked who she was, and she quickly answered in a way that satisfied them.

Upon reaching the area where all the dwellings were located, Lua separated from the group. Thanks to the card she had managed to steal from one of the guards, she went from house to house until she found one with Viktor's name on the sign. This excited Lua greatly, but she didn't expect to find instruments of unusual and primitive torture instead of him. Fear began to grip her as she imagined the tortures and ordeals he might have endured.

She continued walking with her head down, overwhelmed. When she arrived at a dwelling, she read a little sign next to the door on the left side, indicating it was the guest room. Without thinking and exhausted from so much searching, she opened the door, hoping to find Viktor. Instead, she found him surrounded by three guards with rail cannons pointed at a kneeling Viktor.

Without hesitation or asking, Lua attacked them, leaving two guards unconscious on the ground and knocking the last one down with his head touching the ground but leaving enough space for him to speak.

"Who are you?" asked the soldier.

"I am Viktor's girlfriend, and I've come to save him. Do you mind?" said Lua. Viktor's face lit up; it was the first time she referred to their relationship as a romantic one.

"What were you planning to do with Viktor?" Lua continued.

"We were going to ask him about the secrets hidden in the Antler's great dome."

Immediately after, Lua grabbed the soldier's head and let go, saying, "You see, the dome is very weak. It has many underground tunnels, like the one we came through, which are not protected. They are perfect for traversing the city undetected. Also, the dome has no oxygen generation; instead, through microfissures and a single filtration system, the Antlers stay alive. You just need to put an explosive in the only filter, and the entire city will collapse."

Viktor was astonished. He didn't know why Lua was revealing these secrets of the city to Kaki. Suddenly, Lua whispered in his ear, "Your secret will die with you, but your execution will be proof that it will never be revealed again," and she crushed his head with her foot with such force that it crumbled under the pressure.

Chapter 27

"Lukotico, Berto, Gonzalo, and Mafalda disembarked from the transporter several minutes late because the traffic in the sky had been impressive. Upon getting off the transporter, they saw that it was almost impossible to walk through those mud-filled fields, and they needed to hire one of the horses to carry the luggage, which was housed in the cabin opposite the taxi stand.

Each of them rode their pet, and upon reaching the cabin, they encountered a rather unpleasant attendant who served them and offered the horse in a rude manner, although they eventually managed to buy it at a very good price. They loaded all their bags full of belongings and clothing onto the horse's back and set off.

Upon arriving at the kingdom's main square, they could see that there weren't as many Samiz in that kingdom as in other kingdoms; there were too few people. However, that didn't matter to them as they remembered their task: to find the chosen one. Contrary to what Lukotico initially thought would be a boring day, it turned out to be intriguing because by mid-morning, he saw some high-ranking soldiers not riding horses but unicorns and pegasi.

It was impressive to see those mythological creatures, twice the height of a person, not including their majestic wings, which were a sight of their own. Mafalda and Berto separated from the group, holding hands under the pretext that with so many people, they could get lost. They arrived at the market; this time, Berto was right as it was teeming with stalls.

They decided to buy various fruits for the animals and themselves and had to go to the meat section. Mafalda thought it would be best to split up for a moment so she could go fetch the meat while Berto took care of the fruit. Lukotico had given them both some money. Berto noticed that the market was heavily guarded by quite a few security personnel, but he decided to continue shopping. After finishing the purchase, he went in search of Mafalda.

That girl produced intense butterflies in his stomach; her personality attracted him because, like him, she was very outgoing and determined, knowing what she wanted and pursuing it obstinately. These qualities drew him to her, aside from her physique. Despite being a bit more robust than usual, her physique was enviable, and Berto knew it. When they reunited, they held hands again and decided it would be best to find Lukotico and Gonzalo when a captain approached them.

"Good morning, documentation please." "We've just arrived in this great kingdom from the Horn Kingdom, and we haven't had time to get our documents, excuse us." "Towards that direction are the offices where you can get your documents. Good luck and have a nice day." "Likewise." As they turned around, they saw a jet-black Pegasus, with the captain riding on its back.

Suddenly, they heard a shop attendant shout, and then they saw a boy running out of the store with a bag of fruit. The captain went after him, and Berto looked at Mafalda, indicating that he should help her, and so he did. Berto dashed in the direction of the boy. Berto had so much adrenaline that he had no trouble keeping up with the Pegasus and even surpassed it in speed.

When he caught up with the boy, Berto subdued him on the ground, waiting for the captain to arrive. "Thank you, and well done. Um, what's your name?" "Berto, pleased to meet you." "I'm Natalia, one of the captains of the Union Army." "Pleased to meet you. The Pegasus is beautiful, isn't it?" "Indeed. She was found as a baby in the middle of the forest, disoriented, next to the corpse of her mother who died from mortal wounds inflicted by some animal. It was a horrific scene, one I'll never forget.

But let's not talk about her; it makes me sentimental. What brings you to this kingdom, and why this one?" "Forgive me if it sounds cheesy, but I feel like I had to step out of my comfort zone to find what I'm really looking for. And now that I'm here, I feel disoriented because I can't help but notice how beautiful you are. I hope to have the opportunity to get to know you better."

"Well, what a pity for you. I also want to get to know you better." At that moment, Mafalda arrived loaded with several baskets of fruit and meat. "Berto! Help me!" "I'll be right back, Captain." "Call me Natalia." Berto approached Mafalda to help her; he grabbed one of the baskets she was carrying while Natalia approached to greet Mafalda.

"Good morning, we didn't get to greet earlier, but my name is Natalia, and what's yours?" "My name is Mafalda." "Pleased to meet you." "I was telling your husband that this kingdom is very safe, and the Union Army will help with anything you need." "Thank you very much." "Well, I'm off to continue my watch. Goodbye, nice to meet you," said Berto with a mischievous smile.

They both walked towards where Lukotico and Gonzalo were. It was easy to find them; to find the chosen one, Lukotico had summoned Giorgi and transformed him into a very adorable small dog, holding him in his hand while pretending to be blind with closed eyes. Gonzalo followed behind Lukotico, keeping an eye on the people in case something unusual happened.

After searching fruitlessly for several minutes, Lukotico thought it was absurd to continue like this, so he immediately opened his eyes and looked around for Gonzalo, who was a few meters away from him, laughing as he observed him. Lukotico approached him."What? Just killing time?" "That's right." "Where are your brother and Mafalda?" "I haven't seen them around."

"Well, I'm seeing them right now, and with the number of people around, there's not even a breath of space between them because they're so close." "How so?" Gonzalo turned around and saw his brother and Mafalda staring deeply into each other's eyes while their mouths were connected in a long and passionate kiss. When they finished, they separated, both exhausted. Looking towards where Lukotico and Gonzalo were, they found them with their mouths open, astonished."

Chapter 28

"Viktor didn't understand what had just happened. He had seen Lua kill three men in the blink of an eye and still didn't know how she had done it. He remained in shock. She approached him and gave him a hug followed by a long kiss. "I missed you," Lua said. "Yeah, me too." "We don't have time." "We need to save my parents." "Come on, 'boyfriend.'"

"I'm coming, Lua."Next, I handed Lua another cartridge for the image-changing device, and we left the village, this time walking hand in hand. When we reached the camp's limit, Lua suggested I throw a small energon grenade towards the camp to erase any evidence of what happened there. So, I grabbed a small energon grenade from my pocket and tossed it. The grenade exploded in the air, creating a space vacuum that compressed all matter and then expanded, resulting in an explosion much larger than any conventional grenade.

The camp exploded, and several camp members tried to run, but at that moment, Lua grabbed the railgun pin from my waist, enlarged it, and then started firing at the civilians and soldiers coming out of the camp. I forced her to leave the area immediately. Time was not on our side for my parents, and we couldn't waste it on those poor people. We entered one of the tunnels nearby.

I released my reconnaissance drones into the duct to document the tunnels for me to find a safe path based on the information they gathered. Once the path was mapped, we followed it. My parents were close. The tunnel was wide but not very tall, so we had to crouch. After several hours of walking, we arrived at a large room filled with screens showing Citadel cameras. We were initially startled and frightened as we didn't know where we had ended up, so we hid.

After a while, a mythical creature, a small troll named Champi, emerged from a secret door and sat in a chair, inspecting the cameras one by one. When he spotted us crouched due to one of the cameras pointing directly at us, the troll stood up and started searching for us, saying, "Whoever you are, I won't harm you. I'm Champi." We had been caught, and the only way out alive was to negotiate with this Champi.

"Good afternoon, we're Viktor and Lua. We apologize for intruding, but the tunnel we followed led us here," I said. "All good tunnels pass through me; I designed them," Champi replied. "Did you build the tunnels?" "Indeed, young man. I could say I'm the founding father of Antler Citadel." "A pleasure. Whose child are you?" "Well, truth be told, my father is Halfonso Valtorium, the grand master of the citadel." "I coincided with him in its creation; your father is an excellent specimen. I don't think he remembers me," I said. "Thank you, but right now, we have a problem.

My parents have been captured, the sages have them locked up, and we planned to save them. Can you help us?" "Of course, for

Halfonso, I'll do anything. Come here," Champi said, pointing at his more than a hundred computers. We approached the computers, and Champi pointed out a specific screen where we could see my parents chained to a wall.

Both bodies were malnourished and showed signs of physical violence, likely from the sages. I felt powerless; not being able to do anything to save them made me nervous. After thanking Champi for his help and promising to visit him again, we followed a tunnel Champi recommended to quickly reach the dungeons. Later, from the tunnel, we started hearing noises from the surface.

We shuddered but continued walking. The tunnel was high enough to walk comfortably. Lua started running; she seemed happy, and I didn't know why. The situation was unsettling at least. I was nervous, trying to devise a plan to rescue my parents, but that day, I wasn't thinking clearly. I had been beaten badly by Kaki in the morning and couldn't think clearly.

Upon reaching the location Champi had marked on the tunnel map, we saw an obscured trapdoor above us, covered in vines. Lua took out a knife she had taken from one of the guards earlier and began cutting the vines. One by one, she freed the trapdoor from the plants until it was completely uncovered. Then, I started turning the latch of the trapdoor until it opened, creating a loud noise.

Upon opening it, we saw that the trapdoor connected to one of the fortress's storerooms, so we took the opportunity to grab a bite. When I tried to use another cartridge for the image-changing device, I realized I was out of cartridges. I thought it best to proceed without getting caught, but Lua had other plans. She believed a swift attack was the best option to rescue my parents as soon as possible.

Without giving me time to find an alternative, Lua dashed out of the room, and I followed. At the entrance, I saw a guard lying unconscious on the floor; it was probably Lua's doing. I took out the map Champi had given me and plotted the quickest route, then followed it.

Every corner I turned, I found unconscious guards where Lua must have been, but I couldn't see her anywhere. After running through corridors for 20 minutes, I finally saw Lua. She was surrounded by ten guards, seemingly unconcerned about the uneven odds.

She grabbed one of the guards with immense strength, flipped him, and used him as a bat against the other guards, incapacitating them. One by one, she finished them off to clear the way for me. I tried to greet her, but suddenly, in the distance, I saw the captain of the sages' personal guard approaching atop a Leviathan, their ancestral pet."

Chapter 29

The couple approached Lukotico and Gonzalo, but they noticed that both were holding hands. It was already official, thought Lukotico. The affection both felt could be seen in the eyes of the couple. Gonzalo, visibly affected with teary eyes as if on the verge of crying, was the first to speak. "Is there something you want to tell me?" "This wasn't supposed to happen this way, but since we're here, the truth is yes, little brother. As you might have noticed over the past few days, Mafalda and I have been acting strangely. The reason is that we've committed to being together as far as love guides us. I hope this doesn't pose any inconvenience for you, Lukotico."

"Not at all. Passion combined with love is powerful, and if you know how to channel it correctly, you can significantly increase your strength. But for that, you must train hard," replied Lukotico. "We will, my lord." "Please don't call me that. I'm just a humble servant of my mission; I don't deserve such formalities." "What do we do first?" asked Mafalda, a bit lost as it was her first quest. "Berto and Gonzalo will search the streets together, while you and I will look for shelter."

"Perfect, let's go," responded all three. As planned, the group split into two again, leaving the sibling couple with the difficult task of searching for the chosen one in those domains. The first pair, composed of the siblings, decided that since they had already been to the market before, there was no need to return. Thus, they preferred to go to the fair, which was currently taking place on the outskirts of the kingdom. Upon arriving at the fair, they saw demarcated zones, each marked for different kingdoms.

It was an international fair of realms, a kind that only took place every 500 lunar cycles, making it a miracle to be there. They explored stall by stall until they reached a jousting tournament where a knight from the Horned Kingdom was facing another from the Volcanic Kingdom. The latter was riding a white horse while his opponent was on an impressively large brown boar.

Both opponents bowed before Emperor Ferro in the royal box, followed by the royal salute. The knights clashed their shields as a sign of respect, and the joust began. Meanwhile, a minstrel named Luis was telling jokes next to Berto. "What do you call a knight who always loses in medieval jousts? Sir Rendered!" "I have another one. Why can't knights play chess? Because they always move the horse."

Gonzalo started laughing, while Berto remained serious until the last joke. "What does a knight do when he loses a tournament? He 'launches' into drinking." Berto grabbed Gonzalo's arm and asked him to move away because it wasn't safe to be so close to the fence. At that moment, one of the knights from the Volcanic Kingdom fell towards the fence, precisely where the siblings had been seconds before."Close call," said Gonzalo."Let's get out of here," demanded Berto.

"Let's go find Lukotico; hopefully, they've already found a place to rest. I'm very tired; the journey has been exhausting. I don't know how you managed to get some rest in the taxi.""You know I can sleep anywhere, anyhow; it's a skill, to be honest," concluded Berto.The sibling pair separated from the group of people and began their search for the other couple, hoping to rest and eat something in the first establishment they found. They weren't picky about that; when you're hungry, food is always just food.

Chapter 30

"Lukotico and Mafalda kept walking without success. Since it was a holiday, everything was closed, including taverns. But they didn't give up yet; instead, they continued searching through the streets. Finally, they found a hostel, or so it seemed because the owner of the establishment was at the entrance with keys in hand. As they approached to ask if they could request a room, the owner replied that at that moment, the hostel was closing. Disheartened, they continued their search.

"Mafalda, are you happy?" Lukotico asked discreetly."To tell you the truth, I haven't experienced complete happiness yet, only temporary happiness. But to answer your question, I am happy now. Berto makes me very happy.""That's why I asked, now privately, if you're truly happy with him. Your happiness is my happiness, but only if it's complete."

"Don't worry, we'll reach complete happiness one of these days. We're still getting to know each other, and I'm a bit shy and hesitant in that aspect. Please give me some time."At that moment, they saw the twins approaching them with a desolate look."We haven't found the chosen one, I'm sorry," said Gonzalo.

"Well, actually, we might have found him. We heard about a comedian named Luis, who stood out from the rest of the people," said Berto."Now that you mention it, it's true. Luis might be the chosen one, but we won't know until you come and check for yourself," said Gonzalo."Fair enough, we may have let you down. We couldn't find any hostel to stay in, I'm sorry."

"Today was a holiday, it would have been a miracle if we found any hostel or tavern open," said Mafalda."So, since there's no place to sleep, why don't we all go together to see this comedian and find out if he's the chosen one or not? What do you think of the idea?" Lukotico suggested."Agreed," replied Berto."Okay," replied Mafalda and Gonzalo.

Together, they headed back to the fair.As they reached the fair, the sirens all over the city began to sound an alert, and unaware of why, they kept walking. Unintentionally, they found themselves surrounded by a herd of dark orbs, which were actually soldiers with spears in their tiny arms, staring at the group unfriendly. They looked towards Lukotico, seeking some kind of response.

"Friends! Listen to me closely, for I speak from the depths of my heart. You are the chosen ones, the most powerful beings in this world. And I don't say this as mere flattery, but because I know that within each of you, there burns a flame that makes you shine like the sun in the sky.But to achieve your full potential, to honor your greatness, you must unite your souls and reach the core of your energy. Only then can you fight as one, as if connected by an invisible bond that makes you invincible.Because yes, my friends, you are the chosen ones. And your destiny is in your hands.

So go forth, lift your heads, and shine with all your splendor. Let the whole world witness and bow before your greatness!"They all joined hands, forming a circle among themselves, while Berto and Lukotico watched them hopefully.

Each of them began emitting a different light from their bodies until the rays of light from all of them intertwined, rising to the sky in a spiral of colors while forming a shield of light that prevented the soldiers from penetrating it. Lukotico was thrilled, and Berto cheered for his companions, especially for Mafalda.At that moment, Lukotico placed Giorgi on the ground and suggested that he transform into what he had always wanted to be and had been insisting on Lukotico for a long time.Giorgi obeyed and began to increase in size gradually.

His front legs shrank, feathers emerged all over his body, and his jaw enlarged until he transformed into a magnificent, red T-Rex. He crouched down to let Lukotico climb onto his back.Meanwhile, while Giorgi was transforming, Lukotico had handed Berto a flaming sword, saying, "Let the light guide you."The chosen ones began creating a shield of light around themselves, causing the dark orbs to vanish upon contact but weakening the shield.

The rest of the soldiers advanced mercilessly towards the chosen ones. So Lukotico and Berto's task was to protect the chosen ones with the weapons they carried.They fought for several tens of minutes until their bodies started to tire and wear out from the battle, and they found themselves surrounded by the orbs of darkness.When they saw there was no escape, they witnessed the orbs turning their backs, as an army of union soldiers made their way towards them, led by the army captain, Natalia.

She rode a white horse while wielding a considerably sized war axe in her hand. All the union soldiers were clad in primary silver armor with secondary blue color, while Natalia wore secondary yellow armor."Thank you for your patience," Natalia said, addressing the group. "We're here to help. Together, we shall overcome this darkness and restore peace to our land."With the reinforcements from the union soldiers, they engaged in a fierce battle against the dark orbs, combining their strengths to push back the opposing force. Together, they fought bravely, striving to bring an end to the chaos that had engulfed their world."

Chapter 31

Viktor could see from afar as Lua dodged the Leviathan's first attack, but the second one struck her directly in the stomach, sending her hurtling at high speed toward the wall behind her. He couldn't let that monster finish her off, so he shouted at the top of his lungs with all the strength his vocal cords could muster. The creature stopped looking at Lua and focused on him, while he prepared to flee the scene.

The monster turned toward him, disregarding the orders shouted by its rider, gaining momentum and launching itself toward Viktor. He began to run through the corridors he had been through before, buying time for Lua to recover from the impact. At a certain moment, he managed to shake off the creature, so he cautiously made his way back to where Lua had been lying on the ground.

Upon arrival, he saw that there was no one there, neither Lua nor any guard. He was confused. Where could Lua be now? Captured? After several seconds of contemplating what to do, he decided to search for his parents; they would know what to do. He glanced at the piece of paper, the map, that Champi had drawn for him to navigate through the building. After checking the directions, he dashed off, hoping not to encounter any guards. Upon reaching the kitchen, it was empty.

What he didn't expect was that the adjacent room, the war room, which had always been guarded during his previous excursions, was now without any security guards watching over it. He continued his path, now nearing the dungeons. He descended the spiral stairs to the lower floor and was surprised to see the number of cells in the dungeons, all filled with prisoners. He spent quite some time searching through the maze-like corridors of the dungeon, hoping to find his parents in one of the cells.

After much anguish, he managed to find them in cell 666, alongside two more prisoners, who coincidentally happened to be two sages, part of the council of sages. Upon seeing him, his mother jumped with joy from her metal cot and ran toward where he was, hindered only by the metal bars separating them. He quickly looked for a way to force the lock, but it was impossible with the means he had. Thus, he sought advice from his father, who, disregarding the situation, began to tell a story from their past.

On a sunny day in the desert, about 300 centuries ago, something unexpected emerged from the sand: a small cherry blossom branch, pink. To give you some context, in that desert, they hadn't seen a drop of water for a long time; it never rained, and due to that situation, no flora had grown as far back as their memories could recall. Thus, the people of that era were incredulous about this event.

After 50 years of growth, that cherry blossom gradually became the hope of the people because it could only mean one thing: the drought was finally going to end. Every day, dozens of townspeople gathered around the cherry blossom and made requests, as if it were a deity, to the extent that temples were built in honor of the tree, then called Bioç. Annually, its fruits were collected and planted in the arid desert soil in hopes of more like it. As often happens, after several years of following this method, some grew tired of the tree and wasting the little food they obtained, planting it uselessly.

Thus, demonstrations were called to harvest the tree's fruits and feed the needy; many people turned away from the religion for this reason, and their faith faded without results. One day, the tree split open at its trunk, revealing a wooden door. From within emerged a being resembling a townsman, the first Antler. He introduced himself as Omega, explaining to the townspeople that his species, the Antler, had rebelled against the tyrant Zyon Vexar, leader of the Renegade system. They had expelled them from the system, and they had to flee. Unluckily, their colonial ship was intercepted by space pirates.

They were forced to separate onto different planets, and he had landed there. After recounting his story, he requested help to repair his signal transmitter to call his own kind. In return, he would offer them his knowledge. Upon acceptance, Omega created a staff with a pink stone at its tip. With the staff, he touched the ground, and the earth trembled. Each of the seeds that the townspeople had planted began to bloom, creating a completely new landscape in a matter of days.

This new environment allowed the townspeople to advance technologically for many years while also attempting to repair the transmission antenna unsuccessfully. It took several years until the antenna could be properly repaired. After that, Omega contacted his people, inviting them to his location.Gradually, dozens and dozens of ships appeared daily in the sky of that place. Little by little, the settlement of the Antler and the townspeople flourished happily, cooperating together.Unfortunately, one day, Omega died in an aerial accident while trying to assist an Antler ship.

After the incident, the Antler blamed the townspeople for the aerial accident, but neither his staff nor his body was ever found. It was said that they exploded along with the ship, but it was never confirmed.Your mother, several sages, and I have been searching for years for the staff because it holds unprecedented power that can help us reunite with the Samiz.The problem arises from the other sages not agreeing with this quest, feeling it is counter-revolutionary.

That's why they've imprisoned us. Son, it's no use getting us out of here. Go to our office and investigate the whereabouts of the staff. Only a person with a pure heart can wield the staff; when you are close, the staff will guide you to its location. But first, you must save Lua; she's too important for you to let her die like this. Meet up with Axiom; he will know what to do.

I will do that, thank you.After bidding farewell to his parents, shedding a few tears, Viktor left the cell area through the same path he took before to reach there.As he ran, he tried to pay attention to every sound, hoping it might help him find Lua. But it was in vain; he didn't find her anywhere in the castle. Upon exiting the castle, feeling defeated, he noticed at that moment how the right tower exploded, releasing a large plume of smoke. Quickly, he made his way towards the tower, as that could be the signal he had been waiting for.

As he ran, he saw that the fallen soldiers had disappeared. Hastening his pace even more, this time he followed the traces of blood to see where they led. He reached a gigantic room overflowing with soldiers. Luckily, he had entered through one of the balconies, not the main door, which was guarded by several security guards. After observing the scene for several minutes, he saw the guards moving aside, making space for a sage who was accompanied by a chief guard. In the center of the room was a semicircular oval door emitting a blue light.

From it emerged two men, one dressed in black armor with fluorescent yellow figures, and the other man wore a more modest armor, red and black, with a single symbol on it, representing the Teherita flag. He knew the sage; his name was Santhiago, one of the three most important sages of the Antler, whose position was above that of the grand master, his father's rank. As they were all silent, their conversation was audible. Welcome to the dome. Thank you, Santhiago, replied the man in the black suit with a smile. Shall I introduce you to the city? asked the host. I'm sorry, but this isn't a sightseeing visit. We've come for a specific reason, the man in the black suit responded again, removing his helmet to reveal a man whom Viktor knew well, named Luther. His parents had told him many stories about him and his reign of terror with the Night Whispers.

We've found 4 chosen ones thanks to the locator we placed on the Antler. What was his name again? Lukotico Hektor chimed in. Thank you, Hektor. So, we've built another portal in the realm of the Samiz thanks to the technology you provided, and we've sent entire battalions of troops to get the chosen ones. And what has been the result? Santhiago asked. The twenty-fourth battalion was destroyed, and the thirty-third retreated from battle. According to the reports I received, wave after wave, they're destroying my army. They've managed to create a shield capable of withstanding our attacks.

Don't forget Lukotico and his spirit pet; he's finishing off our officers, Hektor said as he removed his helmet. We believe someone here has been leaking information about our plans, Luther continued. We know that; we've already captured them. They're called Halfonso Valtorium and Kerry Xylonis, and we have them imprisoned along with an agitator. If you'll accompany me, gentlemen, the prisoners are over here. Santhiago said cheerfully. Perfect, let's interrogate them, said Hektor with a malevolent smile.

The three of them headed towards a part of the room where there were three iron rings, with prisoners tied by their extremities to these rings. Any movement would cause an electric shock from a staff emitting electrical charges. Upon focusing his sight, Viktor saw that those prisoners were actually his parents, and off to the side, apart from them, was Lua. He couldn't believe it. He had just spoken with them a moment ago, and now they were going to be interrogated. The first to approach was Santhiago.

Hello, Halfonso, how are you, old friend? In a fit of rage, my father spat in the sage's face, immediately being struck with the electric staff by one of the guards. Criminal, we haven't come here to talk but to subdue you. Do you understand that? Luther asked. My father refused to speak, looking angrily at the sage, his face still red from the blow. Santhiago signaled for another guard to strike my father again. I'll ask you just once, how many chosen ones are there, and how do we defeat them? My father refused to answer that intrusive question. Another blow was dealt to his already bloodied body.

Seeing what they were doing to my father, my mother screamed. Stop it! I'll tell you everything, but don't hit him anymore. Lie to us, and you'll die, threatened Hektor.

First, what have you done to my son, Viktor? Give me some information, and I'll tell you where I have your son, Santhiago quickly replied, bluffing. Give me a sign of life from Viktor, and I'll tell you everything you want to know, mother said. Incorrect answer, replied the sage, giving another signal to the guard to shock my father again. He cried out in pain. Okay, okay, I'll talk, if I recall correctly. The prophecy said the following: Six chosen ones you must find, And a wise leader must be shown, and to find the great solutionTo the terrible and grand agitation.

Six chosen ones, of whom there is one leader, right? According to the prophecy, yes. Then, if we eliminate the leader, the rebellion will end, won't it? If you want to believe that, it's up to you. A rebellion started will never die until the opposers fall. So, let's resolve this here and now; who are the ringleaders of the rebellion? We're all leaders of our own rebellion, aren't we? father said exhaustedly. Luther glanced at Santhiago, who approached father and, with his arm, broke both of my father's legs, leaving him suspended only by his arms from the upper part of the metal ring.

I'd rather die here than kneel before you, traitor, father said, looking at Santhiago with angry eyes. At that moment, Luther looked at Santhiago and nodded. Santhiago approached father again, this time seeming to have good intentions. I forgive you, but my spear doesn't, Santhiago said, kicking the weapon out of the guard's hand and, with another kick, thrusting it into my father's right side.

He let out a final sigh, still with a smile in his eyes, and closed them for the last time.My mother let out a scream so loud and piercing that blood began to drip from her lips. I, on the other hand, felt disoriented. Those three beings had just killed my father, and surely, they would soon go after my mother. So, without even thinking, I lunged at them headfirst from the balcony.

Chapter 32

"Natalia approached the group just as Lukotico dismounted his mount to greet her. The chosen ones, exhausted, stopped emitting light and fell to the ground, drained. Good afternoon, sir. I don't believe we've been properly introduced. I am Natalia, captain of the Union army. And you? I'm Lukotico, merely a guide for them. Your pet doesn't seem like a mere advisor.

Giorgi transformed back into a velociraptor and approached Natalia, emitting a fluorescent light. Lukotico and the other attendees noticed this and went to ask Lukotico if this was possible; he confirmed it. Therefore, Natalia coincidentally happened to be not only the captain of the Union army but also, by chance, one of the chosen ones. Natalia, we need to talk privately for a moment. I can't right now. We need to reorganize the city after the chaos caused by this conflict.

How about we meet when the midnight sun is up? Right now, I need to seek a lot of help to finish this task without angering the commander. Don't worry, we'll help you. The sooner we finish, the sooner we can talk, right? Perfect then. But first, you must help me search for where the captured citizens have been taken, whether they've been left somewhere or are in their homes.

From this list Natalia hands over a list with all the names of the city's residents cross out all those who are still alive, and for the rest, find them and give them a proper burial, notifying beforehand, of course. Is that too much work? Honestly, it is, but we're a sizable group, so we'll finish this task quickly. Thanks for entrusting us. Let's go back now.So, after bidding farewell, Lukotico turned around and saw the chosen ones, who were beginning to wake up.

Well, guys, we have a pending task. How are you feeling? For your first time, you did quite well. Do you feel more connected now? Yes, I feel connected to them somehow replied Berto. I can read Berto's and everyone else's thoughts when I touch them, look said Gonzalo while holding his brother's hand. I don't know how you've done this, but this is not in the manuals anymore, so I can't help you here. You'll have to figure it out on your own. Perfect! exclaimed Mafalda.

But not now, later. First, we must search for a couple of missing people after the attack. The sooner, the better. Come together, everyone, I have something to tell you. Lukotico signaled with his hands for them to gather in a circle around him. You see, according to what Giorgi has expressed to me, I'm certain that the army captain, Natalia, is one of the chosen ones, just like you.

That's why I must talk to her explained Lukotico. According to the list, we need to find three people named Samiz: Victor, Luis, and Juan. We'll split into three groups to speed things up. The first group will be formed by Berto and Mafalda, they will search for

Victor. The second group, composed of Gonzalo and Giorgi, will search for Luis, and I will look for Juan. Be careful.

After the explanation, the group split up, each going their separate ways. The first group began searching the market in case Victor had tried to seek cover among the stalls. They searched stall by stall, asking each vendor if they had seen him. Everyone said the same thing: they hadn't seen him, only knew where he used to be, atop the mountain, in his favorite tree, a cherry tree that should have been lush with its characteristic pink leaves at that time of year.

The couple set off toward the top of the mountain. They walked and climbed rock walls to ascend. Berto slipped several times because the ground was made of sandstone and broke upon contact, causing rocks to fall on his feet. Mafalda didn't have such a hard time because she was in front, so when rocks fell during the ascent, they landed on Berto, not her. After a day and a half of journey, they finally reached the top of the hill. And just as they had been told, there was a person there, meditating, dressed as a monk.

They approached him. Good afternoon, excuse the intrusion. Are you Victor? asked Mafalda. Good afternoon, yes, I am Victor. And who are you? the man replied. I'm Mafalda, and this is Berto. You see, the townspeople are looking for you because after the attack, you ran away, and they thought you had been captured. Mafalda continued. The truth is, I ran because, you see, my father used to tell me a story in which when dark orbs reach a village, it is destroyed by these entities, and all the villagers are captured, later to be sold as slaves to ancient beings called Night Whisperers, who collaborate with the Tehritas, a very important mafia.

The monk recounted. I understand. Before we leave, you must sign here to verify that we have seen you handing over the paper with the names, where there was a box with Victor's name this paper is to confirm that you have not disappeared. Perfect, does anyone have a pen to sign? Victor asked. I have one giving Victor a goose feather pen I'm short on ink. Don't worry about that said Victor, piercing the tip of the pen into the tip of his index finger, creating a drop of blood sufficient to sign the paper.

That would be all, thank you concluded Berto. Are you in a hurry? the monk asked. Not right now, do you need any help? Natalia replied, anticipating Berto's complaint, who was about to speak up. Accompany me in this meditation session, please. I could use some company said the monk. Of course Mafalda replied again.

They both sat on either side of the monk, trying to replicate his meditation posture. This task was easy for Mafalda, but it was more challenging for Berto; he didn't have the flexibility to perform the required positions. When he managed to do so, the monk changed his position, causing Berto to sigh in frustration.

Meanwhile, Mafalda discreetly chuckled. After several minutes of relaxation, Mafalda thanked the monk for the meditation session but used the excuse that their friends were waiting for them and they couldn't leave them hanging. They said goodbye to the monk and descended the mountain."

Chapter 33

"On their part, the second group, formed by Gonzalo and Giorgi, had the task of searching for Luis, a comedian, as Gonzalo remembered, from the fair. They began searching around his house, a small wooden hut with a stone chimney reaching the roof. The stove's ash looked recent, but currently, the hut was completely silent. They decided to re-enter the fair, with the idea of finding Luis again, telling jokes to the fair attendees.

However, upon arriving, disillusionment struck them; everything was also deserted. Gonzalo thought that after the attack, all attendees must have fled the fair and barricaded themselves in the castle walls. After sharing his thoughts with Giorgi, they headed towards the castle. Gonzalo was surprised by the scarce number of soldiers in the city, but his shock peaked upon reaching the main wall of the castle, where hundreds of citizens were fighting against the Union's army, aiming to enter the castle.

Gonzalo was frozen by the scene. After a moment of confusion, he saw Natalia in the distance, cornered by several dozens of civilians wielding clubs and stones; Natalia seemed quite frightened.

In a moment of clarity, Gonzalo suggested to Giorgi to transform into something large and make a loud enough sound to grab everyone's attention. And so, Giorgi gradually transformed into a woolly mammoth, emitting a loud sound from its trunk that made everyone turn to look at him.

At that moment, Natalia took the opportunity to regroup with her army while Gonzalo shouted at the top of his lungs for everyone to relax, that the attack had ceased, that they could return to their routine, their work life. In other words, he explained why at that moment, it was absurd to continue trying to enter the castle because the threat no longer existed. After several seconds of reflection, the citizens looked at each other and immediately apologized to the soldiers, helping the wounded to be taken to the medical tents.

Natalia approached Gonzalo, this time alone, without her escort. Giorgi began to revert to his original form."Good afternoon, Gonzalo, right?" Natalia asked."Good afternoon, yes, I'm Gonzalo, Berto's brother," Gonzalo replied."I wanted to thank you firsthand for saving me earlier. Thank you," Natalia expressed her gratitude ."You're welcome, it's my duty. By the way, do you happen to know where someone named Luis, a comedian, is? Have you seen him?" Gonzalo inquired.

"Well, I've seen him before, trying to calm the situation, but right now, I don't know where he'll be. Why don't you start by looking at the medical tents?" suggested Natalia."Thank you. By the way, what I wanted to tell you earlier, Lukotico said that just like us, you are someone special, very special. He will explain it more in-depth, but the summary is this. We must change this world with the help of a few as special as you. You must help us in that task," Gonzalo told Natalia."Well, I have to go, I need to find Luis. We'll talk later. See you!" Gonzalo concluded.

They said their goodbyes. He bent down to pick up Giorgi and put him in one of the large pockets of his outfit and set off to find Luis. He walked and searched through the various and numerous medical tents where both soldiers and civilians were injured due to the attack and protest. He asked one of the doctors in charge of the tents; they were distinguishable from the others due to a golden bracelet on their forearm.

The doctor replied that Luis was located at the far right, patient number 382. Gonzalo headed towards the indicated area, and indeed, upon entering the tent, it was overflowing with injured people, some asleep, others awake. One by one, he asked for the name Luis until he reached the middle of the tent, where there was a person with their head completely bandaged. Gonzalo looked at Giorgi. He asked if he was Luis; there was no response. Gonzalo realized that Giorgi was trying to climb out of the pocket where he was kept. Given the circumstances, Gonzalo nodded and reached his hand down to the pocket, helping Giorgi to emerge.

Giorgi sat on top of the injured person and began to sleep; he was glowing, and Gonzalo, from experience, knew what that meant. Gonzalo sat in a nearby chair. They waited there for several hours, during which they inquired about the condition of the injured from the doctors in the area, but all assumed the injured person was beyond saving. Gonzalo felt hopeless about the situation. He stood up from the chair with the idea of picking up Giorgi again and leaving the tent with him; he would explain the situation of Luis to Lukotico later.

When he touched Giorgi, time stopped. Gonzalo's eyes turned to the purest white while Giorgi's closed. Gonzalo underwent a kind of transition; he felt as if in a tunnel, completely dark. Suddenly, he heard a voice, coming from the entire room; the room suddenly illuminated, showing Gonzalo a man, with white hair, middle-aged."Good afternoon, chosen one, I am Zenith," said the man."Good afternoon, I'm Gonzalo. Where am I?" Gonzalo asked, his voice altered."Don't worry, you're in an ancestral reality," the man tried to reassure Gonzalo."Have I died?" Gonzalo asked.

"No! On the contrary, Giorgi has chosen you as a worthy successor to the Antler's knowledge. You should feel proud; only choose those pure of heart," announced Zenith."Okay, but who are you?" Gonzalo asked again."Oh, sorry, I forgot to introduce myself. I am the narrator of all the Antler knowledge; the first Antler created me to guide all the chosen ones and show them their full potential. Sounds good, doesn't it?" Zenith replied."Yes, but I have a question.

Can I talk about you with the other chosen ones and with Lukotico?" Gonzalo asked."Of course, talk about me to those you trust. Although my knowledge is better not shared with Lukotico; he's not a chosen one, and what I'm about to teach you now shouldn't be known by anyone other than the chosen ones," Zenith suggested."I understand," said Gonzalo."Well, today, seeing that one of the chosen ones is injured, should we not save him? So today, you will learn how to save someone.The first thing you need to know is that all the powers I teach you, others can also use, and if you combine them, you will enhance them much more than if used separately.

After saying this, place one hand on top of the other, making an X, then place your hands on the chest of the injured person and say these words aloud: 'aliki eni'," said Zenith."Thank you," Gonzalo thanked."Earlier, I saw how you defended against a wave, and you created a kind of shield. In reality, that was light in its most primitive form. You all must learn how to use light to your advantage.

It's simple; today, you'll also learn a new power. In this case, you must learn that each of the chosen ones controls a different power, which can be: control of the elements, object creation, necromancy, animal control, creation of dimensional portals, and the last chosen one has the ability to use the mind and manipulate it. The leader of the chosen ones has a very special power, the ability to manipulate sound and transformation into other beings, like the astral animals do. You all have the power of light, but you must discover what your pure and primitive power is.

So, for now, I will teach you basic powers. The next power is for traveling at the speed of light. It will be useful for you to reunite with the rest of the group before the next attack hits the kingdom. Concentrate on a fixed point with your eyes closed and merge with the light; it will show you what you need to see to guide you. Now it's time for you to go; the doctors will think something happened to you. Practice with your new powers and find your primitive power. See you later!" Zenith concluded.

Gonzalo woke up suddenly from the dream, sweating. He looked back to where Luis had been before, and after several seconds of thinking about how to position his hands, he placed them on Luis's chest and uttered the words softly. "aliki eni," Gonzalo said. Nothing happened. He tried again and again. Giorgi approached him, and upon touching Gonzalo, he felt a surge of new energy. He tried again, with Giorgi in his arm. This time, a powerful green wave emerged from his hands, causing Gonzalo to fall backward, losing balance.

Several minutes passed, and Luis still didn't wake up. But after a while of waiting, Luis began to move his fingers while slowly regaining consciousness. Gonzalo approached him, helping him sit up and removed the bandages from his face, revealing his completely healed face."Thank you very much for saving me! I'm Luis, nice to meet you," Luis expressed his gratitude.

"Pleased to meet you, Luis. I'm Gonzalo. I'm sorry I can't introduce us properly, but we're expected; there's no time to waste. Come with me," Gonzalo said."Where are we going then?" Luis asked."To meet Lukotico," Gonzalo replied."Who is Lukotico?" Luis asked."Lukotico is my guide; he'll know what to do with you. You'll see. Besides, according to Giorgi, you're just like me, someone very special. Come on, cheer up, don't put on that long face; we still have a long journey ahead where we can talk. Let's leave this tent," Gonzalo replied.

Both exited the tent; the doctors looked at Luis with astonishment because he had been a hopeless case just a moment ago. Some knelt before them, thinking Gonzalo was a kind of deity. Gonzalo asked Luis to hold onto him as tightly as possible because they were going to move a bit quickly.With Gonzalo carrying Giorgi in his arm and Luis on his back, it presented a grotesque scene, worthy of being remembered by those present. Although they hardly had time to look, as in the blink of an eye, Gonzalo began to run at the speed of light, making it impossible to keep track of him.It took several minutes to arrive where Berto and Mafalda were waiting, in the market square, the meeting place after completing the task."Good afternoon, everyone.

It's a spectacular day today, you'll all agree with me, won't you?" Luis affirmed as he got off Gonzalo's back. "There are storm clouds on the horizon," Gonzalo asserted. "Why, brother?" Berto asked. "I have a lot of news, and not all of them are good. It's better if we sit somewhere," Gonzalo told them. The four of them sat on benches located at one end of the square; the seats were made of stone but comfortable enough to sit for a while."

You see, I went to find Luis; he was very badly injured in one of the medical tents. I asked the doctors, and they told me he was terminal, to leave him alone. I tried to revive him with healing herbs I had been collecting along the way, a recipe from the orphanage. But nothing worked.

I was about to leave when suddenly, by touching Giorgi to take him with me, I entered a kind of trance, where I had a conversation with someone who called himself Zenith. He introduced himself as a narrator of all the Antler stories; he told me he would help me develop my powers and told me that each of us has a pure primitive power, and each one is different. I still don't know what mine is.

Later, he taught me how to create a healing power and a power to travel at the speed of light. For the healing power, we have to cross our hands," Gonzalo made a cross with his hands, "and say the words 'aliki eni.' It didn't work for me the first time, but if I said them while touching Giorgi, my power increased, and I was able to finally unleash the power. He told me that Gonzalo was interrupted by a shout from a young man approaching them, shouting, "Elected ones! Lukotico has been captured, and they're going to sell him," the young man said.

Chapter 34

"Viktor leapt, his bare arms outstretched; he hadn't thought of any plan, just to finish them off. As he fell, he recalled words from the primitive Antler language, remembering having read them in some book. What was it called? Viktor pondered .He had to recall back to the time when his father gifted him a book containing ancient terms, believed to make the chosen ones special beings. At that time, they didn't believe in the chosen ones, but still, he read the book; it was short, about 20 pages. He remembered some words, classified as dangerously offensive, which he repeated at that moment.— 'Ignis Caelestis!' I shouted at the top of my lungs.

A sphere of light formed around me, it was gigantic, like some sort of bubble, and I braced for the best. Luckily, upon impact, the sphere imploded, leaving everyone in the room blind for several seconds. It was enough time for me to grab the spear they had used to kill my father and, in a mix of rage and vengeance, I plunged it into Santhiago's abdomen, the sage who had executed my father.As everyone regained their senses, they first saw me and then turned their gaze to Santhiago, who was falling to his knees, spitting blood and cursing me. Luther, on the other hand, turned his gaze towards me.

'Capture him! I want him alive!' Luther demanded. I had no intention of fighting, as they outnumbered me, so I ran through the entire room. I looked at my mother and Lua, tears in my eyes, and promised them that I would come back for them. A couple of dozen guards chased after me, each carrying a spear in one hand and a whip in the other. I didn't know what to do; I couldn't leave them to their fate, and I couldn't confront them alone. So, the only thing that came to mind at that moment was to return home and devise a plan there. I ran upstairs, speeding through hallways.

Glancing back for a moment, I realized I was running at the speed of light and had left everyone behind; I had thrown them off. I arrived home, sweating and panting. Creating that ball of light had drained me. I went straight to the shower, taking a long one. As a blanket of steam covered every pore of my body, I reflected on the day's events; too many things had happened. Afterward, I closed all the shutters in the house to avoid being seen. I had dinner with whatever I found, a couple of crispy seaweeds, smoking them slowly to keep them warm.

Then I went to bed, but not before feeding Orca; she hadn't eaten in almost two days, so this time, she devoured all the food I gave her. The next morning, I woke up sweaty, all the sheets rolled up; most likely, I'd had a nightmare that night. I had seen how, after I left the room, they executed both my mother and Lua as an act of revenge, on Luther's orders. That reality haunted me for most of the day, and I felt guilty. By evening, as the sun descended and the street lights dimmed, I left the house. For the occasion, I chose an outfit that wasn't too conspicuous but also not camouflaged. I walked the streets; I had a plan but needed allies. First, I went to Pedro's house; after explaining my plan, he and his brother joined the team. Then we went for Álvaro and Santi; Santi's brothers also joined the group.

To finish, we went to Lua's house; her parents welcomed us with open arms, excited as Lua had disappeared for them, and I had forgotten to inform them. Upon entering their house, we went straight to the living room. I had to explain my plan to everyone; coordination was crucial for everything to go smoothly. 'Before explaining the plan, let me tell you what happened to me yesterday.'

First of all, Lua and I had a mission: to rescue my parents because they were captured by the sages, accused of treason. Lua and I went through the tunnels towards the sages' palace, where they were held prisoner. In the tunnels, we met Champi, an ally. Later, upon entering the palace, Lua had to defeat many guards, but unfortunately, she was captured. Meanwhile, I descended to the dungeons and spoke with my parents. I couldn't free them, but they told me something essential: they were working to find a kind of staff that belonged to the first Antler, named Omega. My father tasked me with retrieving the staff and defeating the sages with it. The problem arose when, upon leaving the dungeons, I heard an explosion from one of the towers.

I quickly turned back and went up to the tower; no one was there, and I was bewildered. I went to the main hall because I heard some noise, and do you know what I found? Luther, the leader of the Night Whispers, Hektor, of the Terithites, along with Santhiago, the sage. I realized when I looked toward the center of the room, there was a portal, and beside it, in one of the wings, there were three prisoners: my parents and Lua. Luther, Santhiago, and Hektor discussed their plans and went to interrogate them.

My father argued with them and was executed. I was in one of the balconies above the main hall. As an act of revenge, I descended to where the three executioners were and just like they had executed my father, I executed Santhiago. I fled the place without being able to rescue either my mother or Lua. So, I'm asking for your help, friends; we must rescue them and confront the sages.

Therefore, my plan is as follows: we'll form three groups. The first will be responsible for stealing guard uniforms so the second group can camouflage themselves in the palace. The second group must seek other allies in the dome, ones who also oppose the corrupt sage regime. Finally, the third group will be tasked with searching my parents' manuscripts and searching for the staff. These tasks aren't easy, but I trust you.' Viktor concluded.

Everyone looked at me with sadness; some even offered condolences. They asked me several questions, which I answered confidently; I had everything well-prepared and thought out. Except for Pedro's question, 'What will we do with Luther and Hektor?' I had no answer for him and replied that we would improvise as we went along. We split into three groups: the first composed of Alvaro and Lua's parents, the second formed by Santi and his two brothers, and the last group, to which I belonged, comprised Pedro, his brother, and myself. I told them that we would meet again at the same time the next day, at Lua's house, and from there, head into the unknown.

But before that, I had a task: tailored suits for everyone. The suits had to withstand blows and energy weapon shots. After saying goodbye, I headed home.Arriving home, I saw that the area was cordoned off with energy shields, preventing access. The door to my house was open, with several officers inside, searching everything. I was scared at first, but then I remembered a phrase from one of the books that startled me. It said: 'The limits of your thoughts are the limits of your world.'So, just as I had done before in the main hall, I concentrated and delved deep into my spirit until I reached the core of my power, and I started walking toward the shield.

I was afraid; if my body touched anything from the shield, I would disintegrate, but I continued forward.Upon touching the shield, it opened, allowing my body to pass through it. I bypassed the officers and quickly entered my room. I closed the door from inside and tried to make as little noise as possible. I gathered all my equipment, but before leaving, I tried to communicate with Lukotico through the mirror. Initially, he didn't respond, but after several attempts, I got an answer.'Lukotico, long time no see. How are you? I'm not doing well here,' Viktor said sadly.

'Well, things aren't going too well here either. I'll tell you, I'm currently imprisoned,' Lukotico replied with a laugh. 'Listen, I'll say it quickly to make it hurt less, or at least I hope so. One day, they arrested my parents, so Lua and I tried to rescue them. We failed, and they captured Lua. Luther, Hektor, and a sage named Santhiago do you know him? killed my father. In vengeance, I killed Santhiago, fled, and was chased by too many.

Also, something very strange happened to me: when I tried to rescue Lua and my mother, I created some kind of light shield and ran at the speed of light. How is that possible? How did you end up there?' Viktor asked. 'Well, one day, we were attacked by an army belonging to Luther. Later, they assigned us several tasks, including finding some missing persons. I had to find a guy named Juan. We formed groups, and I was supposed to go alone. It seemed like an easy job, but it got complicated. Let me tell you,' Lukotico began narrating his story.

Chapter 35

"Luther was furious; right before his eyes, they had killed one of his allies, and a chosen one had appeared and managed to escape. That was unacceptable. He approached Hektor and whispered a couple of contradictory orders, as one required both prisoners to remain alive while the other order suggested execution at the slightest movement. Suddenly, without prior notice, as it should be when someone crossed the portal, a messenger emerged from the portal. He carried a very important message, or at least that was the feeling given his exhausted appearance.

"Your Excellency, I bring a message from the forty-fourth battalion," said the messenger. "Go ahead, what is it about?" Luther said as the messenger approached to whisper in his ear. "Well, they claim to have captured Kerry Xylonis's very own son, the eldest one, a certain Luko, I mean Lutokito, that's his name, something like that," whispered the messenger.

"Good, finally some good news," Luther affirmed happily. "They also request instructions. Several assault battalions are already at the location, awaiting your orders to initiate an attack against the chosen ones," the messenger requested.

"Yes, of course. Let them attack now. There's no time to waste. Instead of three battalions this time, let it be five battalions. Let's see how they handle that," Luther said. "Understood, Your Highness," the messenger bid farewell. Luther ordered Hektor to bring Kerry's son before him; he needed to see him with his own eyes."

Chapter 36

"Come on, come, sit down and tell us," Mafalda tried to calm the young man. The young man, panting, stumbled closer to them, probably from exhaustion. As he was about to sit down, he fainted from exhaustion, hitting his head hard on the stone bench. Gonzalo and Berto were frightened, thinking he was dead. However, Mafalda approached the young man and laid him on the ground, revealing a serious head injury. If they didn't hurry, they wouldn't be able to save him.

Quickly, Mafalda instructed the others to form a circle around the young man and say the words," Aliki eni," they all shouted at once. The young man was enveloped in a series of healing green rings that lifted him from the ground while the wound on his head began to heal rapidly. When the healing was complete, the rings gently lowered him to the ground, and Mafalda quickly held him to prevent him from falling again.

The young man introduced himself. "Good afternoon, sorry, my name is Juan, I'm the one you sent to find Lukotico. Natalia has explained everything to me; I am at your disposal for whatever you need."Without warning, Natalia appeared on her steed, stopping abruptly in front of them."Chosen ones, we must do something; the entire kingdom is once again surrounded by the orders of darkness. I've counted at least three full battalions of soldiers, but there could be more; not all have arrived yet," explained Natalia.

"Let's get out of here," suggested Luis."We can't. This square is surrounded by orbs. They let me pass because they are allied with the Union Army," said Natalia.Gonzalo had an idea. They all formed a circle, holding hands, and placed Giorgi on the ground to enhance their power. One by one, they began to focus on themselves. Mafalda was the first to show her primal power a green aura formed around her. Luis's was blue, Gonzalo's was red, and Natalia's was pink.

Each of them began to rise a few meters from the ground, their eyes still white. Mafalda's power revealed itself animal control. Luis had the power to create objects, while Gonzalo could control the elements, and finally, Natalia had the power to create dimensional portals. Metaphorically, they activated a metaphorical switch within their powers, allowing them to unleash special abilities against their adversaries. Berto with his sword and Juan with his fists stood around the chosen ones, covering their backs. The first shot came from Gonzalo, who unleashed a concentrated torrent of water, causing several orbs to implode.

This was the signal the Luther's army was waiting for. They began to advance slowly towards them, then, seconds later, they sprinted towards the chosen ones. The chosen ones were outnumbered a hundred to one, but they didn't give up; instead, they continued to unleash their powers, some effective and others not.

Mafalda kept casting powers, but none went where she aimed; they dispersed in the air as if from a sprinkler.

They fought like this until the orbs had completely surrounded the chosen ones, Juan, and Berto. They couldn't do anything until they heard a sound coming from the forest. Moments later, waves and waves of orbs shot up into the sky. Berto and Juan couldn't see the origin, but the chosen ones could. Mafalda was proud her hundreds of deer, boars, elks, bears... had managed to break the ranks of the orb army, filling everyone with hope.

They quickly continued to unleash their powers, each one more powerful than the last. Finally, the hundreds of animals defeated the orbs, giving the chosen ones a much-needed relief. They fell onto a bed of leaves created by Gonzalo to minimize the impact. Berto and Juan had several serious injuries, but with Giorgi's help, they healed quickly. The problem arose when the Union Army approached the square, commanded by Delma.

In total, three complete battalions appeared, all armed with war animals and artillery. Delma approached them in a gesture of peace. "Good afternoon, you are all under arrest in the name of our emperor Ferro. Surrender now or prepare to suffer," announced Delma. They looked at each other in astonishment, without answers. Natalia was the first to speak. "Do you even know what these chosen ones have just done? They saved the city; you should treat them as heroes, not as wretches," Natalia protested. "Regarding that, Natalia, hand over your sword and armor.

You're suspended until further notice from the Union Army, and by order of Emperor Ferro, you've been banished from the kingdom. You have a day to leave the kingdom; say goodbye to your new friends. Thank you for your service; capturing Lukotico has been very useful to us," Delma thanked her.

They all looked at each other, not sure if they had heard correctly what Commander Delma had inadvertently revealed."I'm sorry; don't think badly of me. They set a trap for me; they have my children imprisoned for crimes they didn't commit," Natalia said, crying.Mafalda was the first to sympathize with her and went to hug her. The rest, seeing this attitude, also felt compassion for her, and they all went to hug her together."Delma, give us a minute to gather our things, and we'll go with you. We surrender," Berto said suddenly.

Everyone was astonished, but seeing Berto turn around and wink at them calmed them down. He told them to form a circle around him, and they did."I have a plan; it's simple, it could go very well or very badly, but we must try it. Luis, your pure primal power is to create dimensional portals, isn't it?" asked Berto.Luis nodded."Good, this is what we'll do. You, Gonzalo, create a 360-degree water shield around us so they can't see what we're doing. Meanwhile, Luis, create a portal. It doesn't matter where it leads, as long as we leave this traitorous kingdom." Berto continued.

Everyone agreed with this proposal and started working on the plan. Gonzalo created a three-meter-high and one-meter-wide water shield. Delma shouted at them from the other side of the shield."You can't escape. Hide all you want, but we'll find you, and it will be worse," Delma threatened.To distract them, Mafalda ordered the birds to attack the soldiers. This created a distraction big enough for the soldiers not to hear or see the five-meter-high portal. Luis hadn't calculated the portal's dimensions well; it was his first time.Delma ordered the attack.

The three battalions surrounding the square began the siege, putting their elephants with catapults and crocodiles with ballistae in the front line. They didn't stop shooting projectiles at the chosen ones, while Berto and Juan fought against the soldiers. Natalia had given Juan a samurai katana, which he wielded magnificently.Luis was taking too long to create the portal, and the accumulating fatigue made it increasingly difficult to defend the position.

In the distance, in addition to the Union soldiers, another five battalions of orbs of darkness approached. Berto was surrounded by soldiers who launched themselves at him, immobilizing him. Luis finally managed to create a stable enough portal for them to cross. He told them that in order to set a destination in the portal, he must have been there in person at some point in his life, which ruled out many places such as the dungeons where Lukotico was imprisoned.

The first to cross the portal was Luis himself, followed by Natalia, Mafalda, and Gonzalo. Juan tried to drag Berto through the portal; he was almost dying, suffocated by the soldiers. Finally, after many attempts, he succeeded, dragging his badly wounded body along with several soldiers on top of him. The two jumped into the portal.

Chapter 37

"Viktor found himself in a difficult situation; confronting the sage and attempting to defeat him would give him an advantage in attacking the palace, but it could also lead to his capture, completely cancelling the initial plan. I tried to slide past his legs towards the house's door, but his legs closed abruptly, trapping my neck. I felt a hand grab my hair. "Hello," I timidly greeted. "Good afternoon, but look who we have here, if it isn't Viktor, the youngest son of Halfonso," the man said.

"Leave me alone," I warned the men as the officers approached me to examine me closely. "Calm down, kid, we're friends. We come on behalf of your father. I'm the sage Axiom, and they are Aurora and Nexus. We've come to help you find the staff. You gave us quite a scare; we thought you had been captured," Axiom said. "Aren't all sages corrupt?" I asked. "Well, it seems not," Axiom chuckled. "Well, we must get to work; there's no time to waste. Do you know where your father's plans are?" Axiom asked. "I know they're in the vault, but I don't know how to access it," I said. "I'll take care of that, don't worry," the sage assured me.

Axiom let me go and helped me up. He asked me how I had managed to evade the shield. As I didn't fully trust him, I told him there was a secret tunnel. He accepted my answer but didn't insist. Together, we searched for the door for several hours, moving furniture, charging stations, even starting to remove ceiling panels, but nothing; we couldn't find the way out. At one point, while removing another ceiling panel, I remembered my mother used to come to my room and say that Orca was very special, reaching into the fish tank, touching Orca.

It seemed like a strange gesture to me, but now I understood. I repeated the gesture, and I saw Orca move to the bottom of the tank and touch a button, which caused a staircase to unfold in the living room. Everyone was thrilled; we quickly climbed up to the vault, and indeed, all of my parents' documents were there, including a map indicating where the relic was supposed to be. Studying the map closely, I could see how the path crossed very dangerous places such as the hidden realm of the Night Whisperers, the living smoky forest, or even the Death Pit.

I had to speak with the group immediately; the plans had drastically changed. Axiom promised me official suits the next day, so Group One no longer had any task, and Group Three could begin the journey. Axiom, Aurora, and Nexus bid an excited farewell. I asked them not to remove the shield in case the sages came to attack me; they agreed and closed the door. I ran up to my room and without showering or having dinner, I went to sleep. The next morning, I woke up happy. Despite the changed plans, things were going well, and I liked that.

I grabbed the backpack with all my gadgets and trinkets and left the house. Upon closing the door, I realized I hadn't taken the map, so I went back in and grabbed it. This time, I made sure I didn't leave anything behind upon closing the door. I blended in with the crowd walking the streets until I reached Lua's house, where they were already inside having breakfast, eagerly waiting to begin. Upon arrival, I announced changes to the plan. I told them what had happened the night before. They understood immediately. I told them Group One was now useless, and we needed to eliminate it, so Group One would join Group Three and Group Two.

Lua's parents willingly joined Group Two, while Álvaro joined Group Three. Over the past few weeks, my relationship with Álvaro had plummeted into the abyss, but I still trusted him. We gathered supplies, and Group Three was ready to embark on the adventure. We said goodbye to the second group and entered one of the city's secret tunnels. If any guard saw us leaving the dome, we could consider ourselves exiled, so we had to be very stealthy. The tunnel had a not-so-high water level, a couple of centimeters, but enough to wet our feet if we didn't wear the boots I had crafted for the occasion. Upon exiting the tunnel, we found ourselves in the desert area, where minerals were extracted centuries ago to build the dome. Now, there was nothing left, not even a living being.

I distributed breathing masks and radiation filters to each one of us. If, at any moment, any of our suits were damaged, even just a scratch, radiation would seep through, slowly killing the wearer. That terrified me internally. When we were kids, they told us dying from radiation was one of the worst sensations. Lua's mother, Sonsoles, checked our suits one by one to ensure they were intact. After the check, we began walking; the gravity inside the dome was artificial, but outside, the gravity was different. We made great leaps while walking.

This helped us move swiftly. We were in an eagle formation, with Sonsoles at the front, leading, and right behind her was Lua's father, Mauricio. We walked or hopped for about half a sun approximately. We got tired and stopped to take a break and clean our dust and sand filters.In the distance, we could see the desert coming to an end and the more exciting part beginning, navigating the Night Whisperers, a tribe that, although primitive, outnumbered our army, the Antlers, making it tricky to consider attacking them.

After the break, we continued our march, scaling several sand dunes, and accidentally, Álvaro stepped into quicksand. It seemed like he was doomed to sink due to the speed at which the sand was swallowing him, but Mauricio saved him, grabbing his arm and, after several efforts, managed to pull him out. The march co ntinued.We reached the Forbidden Valley, the supposed residence area of the Night Whisperers, but at first glance, there seemed to be nothing there, not even a simple hut, just mountains.

I encouraged them to keep walking; I had a plan to deal with the sages, which could either go very well or fail miserably, leading to all of us being annihilated.I was looking back to see if anyone was following us when, at one point, I slipped down a hill. When I reached the bottom, I startled, scared, checking my suit for any scratches.

Fortunately, the suit remained perfectly sealed. The problem was that, making so much noise, a patrol of the Night Whisperers intercepted us, aiming energy rifles at us."

Chapter 38

"All of them arrived at an unknown kingdom for almost everyone, the kingdom of the Aquatics, a realm completely immersed in an ocean. And most of the group had never swum before. Berto was badly wounded, Mafalda knelt before him and begged him to keep fighting for his life.

Berto had a spasm, and immediately after, another one. This gave Mafalda hope, and to encourage him to keep going, she spoke kind words about him, describing all the aspects she had fallen in love with. Berto had a much stronger spasm, and when Mafalda was about to kiss him, Berto opened his eyes, met Mafalda's lips, and responded to the kiss. Giorgi approached him and healed the rest of Berto's wounds, Mafalda helped him stand up, and when he managed it after several attempts, she gave him a tight hug. Berto would never forget that, and he also appreciated Mafalda's unconditional love for him, something his parents always said about them.

At least until one day his father went off to war and his mother fell ill. Juan recounted the moment, and Berto approached him to give him a hug and whisper thanks. After the intimate moment, they returned to reality. They had two guards captured; they had been apprehended after jumping into the portal with Berto. He suggested releasing both soldiers because they were far from home, and their mothers would be missing them.

Unanimously, they accepted the proposal. They also debated their situation; they had to save Lukotico above all. But they didn't know how to get back there. They had all their animals in the stable. "Let's not worry about that now. Let's go to sleep; we're all very tired, and tomorrow we'll discuss and find a solution," Juan said, exhausted. Everyone agreed, Gonzalo grumbled a bit but also opposed deliberating at that moment. Together, they summoned a pod of dolphins and rode on their backs to descend to the kingdom of the Aquatics.

They had to hold their breath until they reached the main gate. At the city gate, there was an oxygen bubble, allowing the chosen ones to continue breathing. They were asked who they were, and they made up a story about their father sending them to visit a cousin who lived in the kingdom of the Aquatics and bringing their partners along so that their cousin could meet them.

The guards didn't fully believe the story until Mafalda grabbed Berto around the waist and gave him a tender kiss on the lips. This solidified the story they were telling the guards. They were allowed to pass. Once inside the kingdom, they had to continue using the dolphins to move around the city. The city was gigantic, rumored to be the largest of the six kingdoms, the second most technologically advanced, only behind the Volcanics.

The city was composed of a variety of coral reefs, all different colors, adding splendor to the kingdom. If they looked up, they could see the marine highways, where even newborn seahorses followed along. This surprised the chosen ones since, in their kingdoms, the roads were always chaotic.The palace was located in the center of the city, majestic, painted in rusty pink. Several dozen Union soldiers rode sharks, patrolling around the palace. Looking at the rest of the inhabitants, they noticed they wore a kind of mask covering their noses and mouths, and they thought it might help them breathe through it.

Mafalda looked at Natalia; she was struggling as she had never touched the water before. This situation was new for her, and holding her breath was not her best quality. Gonzalo noticed that near the entrance, there was a small shop selling some trinkets, and among all that junk, they sold breathing masks, third or fourth-hand, but still functional. Each one put on their mask and returned to their mounts.

They got onto the highway, and immediately a Union army guard stopped them. Seeing that they were very lost, the officer came to help, that is, to show them around the city and its features."Wel come to the kingdom of the Aquatics, with our empress Coralina. I'm Diego, the officer in charge of this area. Here, we're all very organized, but we also have a good time. We have several amphitheaters scattered around the city plus thermal current baths; they are very relaxing, you must try them.

Well, where was I? If you look towards the entrance," pointing at the entrance, "you'll see it's the only entrance and exit of the kingdom, mainly for security reasons.As you may have noticed, the palace is located in the center of the city. We have a very generous policy compared to other realms, so the highway passes under the palace for the queen to greet her fellow citizens.On the left wing of the city is the residential area, and on the right wing, you'll find all our science divisions. Would you like to see them?" the guard asked.

"For my part, that's fine. Now that we have the respirators, we can comfortably go around the city," Juan replied, and the rest agreed with him."Perfect then, follow me, let's go!" the officer exclaimed enthusiastically.The officer showed them all the splendor of the city until they reached the AtlantisBio laboratories.

The officer took them to the main entrance, where they met Laura. She was in charge of the experimentation area on the left wing of the laboratory, where, as she explained to those present, they experimented with technologically advanced weapons, even better weapons than those of the Volcanics.They entered through a white service door; according to her, it would be faster this way.

According to Laura, if her boss saw them, it could be a problem since they would be entertained too long; she loved talking to guests. Laura showed them the first prototype of the laboratory, called the diffractor, which served to divide matter into its primary elements, very useful for mineral extraction some time ago. Right after, there was a long showcase of awards, honoring the invention.

In one of the rooms adjacent to the showcase, there were some residents testing new creations. In the first room, as Laura told them, a new recruit was trying an ion weapon, not as strong as those of the Antler's energy, but enough to disintegrate any armor from any Samiz realm.Next, she presented the armor section, some used by the Union army and others by the empress's private army.

Some of them had shields, and others, simply with their colors, reflected their owner.Juan approached the armor; he had been one of the kingdom's blacksmiths and knew about materials. However, at this moment, he couldn't recognize the element used to make that armor; it seemed too advanced. When he asked Laura, she replied that she couldn't give out that information for security reasons. She encouraged them to continue the tour. After finishing the tour, everyone bid farewell, at the laboratory's main entrance.

Diego accompanied them to one of the kingdom's hotels as it was getting dark. The guard promised that the next morning, he would accompany them to the city market and visit the Union army access tests, which Juan was interested in. And so it was, when they woke up, they went down to the hotel's entrance, where Diego was with.

Chapter 39

Viktor was surrounded by a patrol; the rest of the group had managed to stay atop the hill, silently and undetected. The patrol consisted of two advanced soldiers, two regular soldiers, and an officer in charge of the operation."Stop right there, identify yourself, fugitive!" the officer shouted."I'm Viktor, and I'm not a fugitive, I came to talk to you," I said to them."No one comes here unless they are exiled or expelled from the bubble," the officer repeated.

"I have a very important mission and I need your help, please let me speak to your leader," I pleaded."How many more of you are there?" the officer asked.At that moment, the rest of the group peeked over the top of the hill. Lua's father was the first to descend, followed by his wife and Álvaro. They came down with their hands raised."We will escort you to the city; the council will decide what to do with you," assured the officer.

The two advanced soldiers positioned themselves at the back of the convoy, and they advanced slowly but surely. Along the way, we had time to get to know the guards a bit more, especially Sonsoles,

Lua's mother, who insisted a lot to the officer to at least reveal her name.

Finally, she relented, revealing her real name, Astradia. She explained that her people had been too quiet lately due to recent political changes, saying she still didn't know who they had allied with, but there was a ceasefire with us.Suddenly, a high wall came into view. According to the officer, they had been using technology for centuries to shield their cities from possible Antler attacks.

This surprised Mauricio, Lua's father, as they had just collected some news in the newspaper. They reached the city gates, where, through facial recognition by the officer, the gates opened, allowing the convoy to pass through.The city was enormous, composed of various areas, hermetically sealed by energy gates, even more advanced than those of the Antler themselves. The convoy headed straight for the parliament.Waiting for them at the doors were all the city's governors, five in total, named Hugo, Antoine, Meri Karmen, Marivi, and Veronikka.

According to the accompanying officer, they were the ones making all the decisions for the city and were above the High Inquisitor, Luther.As we approached the governors, they didn't treat us like prisoners but as guests, inviting us to enter the parliament, where they would ask us some questions about our situation. We accepted, but the group left me as their representative.Upon entering, I saw a semicircle with dozens of seats occupied by high-ranking officials and civilians.

I sat in a seat that was above the rest but facing the semicircle. When I was given the floor, I introduced myself and made sure everyone could hear me."Good suns to all. Before anything else, let me introduce myself. I am Viktor, son of Halfonso Valtorium and

Kerry Xylonis, I suppose you know them. About a week ago, they were captured by the council of sages."

"To us, what happens within the dome doesn't matter!" interrupted one of the generals. "As I was saying, they were forcibly captured, accused of treason and other slanders. The thing is, a friend and I ventured into their stronghold to try to rescue them. We arrived too late, and my father was cold-bloodedly murdered by one of the puppets of your High Inquisitor, Luther," I tried to continue. "Those are lies!" shouted a civilian, and others booed at me.

"As you've heard, these eyes saw what they saw. As if that weren't enough, they mistreated my mother, and to this day, they still have her as a prisoner. Furthermore, the other day, I spoke with my brother, Lukotico, who was sent to the Samiz realms to free them from Luther's yoke. I come here today to ask for your consideration and to observe together the history of our past, up to the treaty in the convention after the ten-year winter war.

One of the points of that treaty was that neither of the factions, neither the Antler nor the Night Whispers, were allowed to enslave the Samiz; they were supposed to live freely, without our technology or power. And I come to denounce Luther, the High Inquisitor of the Republic of Light, or as you're commonly known, the Night Whispers. Help me to stop Luther, or else the next to be executed by him will be you, I assure you," I concluded my speech.

Everyone present gasped in disbelief. Their highest representative outside had betrayed the principles of the Night Whispers. One of the Night Whispers governors, Marivi, accompanied us to our rooms while they deliberated on future actions and whether they considered my testimony credible and reliable. Each of us had a different room to rest in. I took off the clothes left on the bed and found new, clean clothes. There was a knock at the door.

Still not dressed, I quickly grabbed some underwear, put them on, and rushed to open the door. It was Hugo, and upon seeing him, I was almost in shock. Before, I hadn't been able to see him properly since Marivi had escorted me the entire way, but having him in front of me now, I didn't know what to say; the words escaped me. He was almost two meters tall, pure muscle.

At first, I was scared, thinking about what I might have done wrong for him to come here to tell me something, but I was surprised when he started speaking."Good suns, Viktor, I'm Hugo, one of the five governors of the city. I didn't come because you got into trouble, seeing your frightened face don't worry," I tried to excuse myself, but the words still wouldn't come out of my mouth, "I've just come to tell you a story, to see if you know it.

Before I start, I want to congratulate you on today's intervention; you were magnificent," he smiled, and I blushed, "I expected a less intelligent young man. It's the first time I've had the pleasure of talking to an Antler." "The pleasure is mine." "Oops, sorry, I didn't realize. I caught you at a bad time; I'll come back another time if you want," he asked after examining me completely and seeing that I was alone in my underwear."No need," I said, while my conscience screamed at me to kick him out of the room."Well, it's going to be a long story, I mean," he smiled, "Can I sit here?" he asked, pointing to where I was seated."Sure, I'll make room for you if you want," I offered."What did your father tell you about the first Antler?" he asked."Well, not much.

He said that a being named Omega came from a tree and helped build everything thanks to an artifact, but he died in a space accident, and the artifact was never found," I recounted."In part, that's true, but you weren't told the whole story. The story goes back 300 centuries, when Omega appeared. Yes, he emerged from inside a cherry tree, but only a few investigated that cherry tree my ancestors did.

They investigated it, and guess what? Inside, there was a great city composed of thousands and thousands of individuals, specifically ants.After Omega's death, his body couldn't be recovered because Omega's life cycle was limited by the ant queen mother. One day, the tree began to wither, and it was because the queen mother was dying, as was the entire colony, including Omega, who, legend says, didn't get lost in space but returned home, waiting to be reactivated by a worthy successor of the queen mother.

The artifact you're looking for is called the Staff of Wishes. Legend has it that even before the Antler set foot on the planet, it already existed, probably from some primitive tribe. But there's a secret I must tell you. That staff isn't lost.Remember when I told you that my ancestors investigated the tree? Well, those same ancestors stored it in a secret place, which can only be discovered by a successor loyal to its principles.

My faction has gone several times to the place to see if they could open the artifact, but it has always been in vain. Later, if you come to my office, I'll show you on a map where you should go," he concluded his story.When I got up to open the door for him, he gently grabbed my jaw and whispered in my ear, "This information isn't free; I'll come to collect it."I felt a shiver run down my spine, but it didn't escalate. Hugo left the room, and finally, I was able to close the door.

I was bewildered and had to go talk to the rest about what Hugo had just told me. I ran out of the room, and I saw a guard looking at me perplexed. I checked my body and realized I hadn't changed, so I apologized and hurried back to the room, where I grabbed the first clothes I saw and put them on. Now dressed, I rushed to the room of Lua's parents, who were there with Álvaro. I told them the whole story and proposed that we go for the artifact the next day. They were thrilled with the discovery and accepted eagerly, except Álvaro, who didn't fully embrace the idea. I decided that after dinner, I would go to Hugo's office to ask for help and directions to the artifact's location.

Dinner was served in one of the parliament's halls; the size of the table seemed infinite. We sat with the governors, arranged by Meri Karmen. I had the good or bad luck to dine with Hugo directly across from me. Veronikka and Álvaro sat on either side of me. The dinner began with a toast to our health, and everyone raised their glasses. As we were about to sit, one of the servants spilled some wine on Hugo's shirt. Without saying a word, he took off his shirt, revealing his entire torso, and handed it to the servant.

The main course was smoked duck with honey, followed by a second course of trout with orange, and it ended with dessert, a bowl of freshly harvested strawberries mixed with goat's milk. Throughout the meal, I spoke with Veronikka while Hugo looked at me playfully, gesturing for me to join his game. His look said it all, but I didn't want to play along. As the second course was served, I had to look straight ahead to eat.

Hugo took advantage of this moment to look at me and lower his gaze to where I couldn't see beyond the table. Then he looked up again. He picked up a jug of beer and spilled quite a bit of liquid over his body, making himself stand out even more. Strangely, it seemed like everyone else in the hall had been frozen, no one noticed what Hugo was doing. At one point, in an attempt to avoid Hugo, I started talking to Álvaro.

Hugo took this as jealousy and saw it as a challenge. He stretched his leg out, and Álvaro noticed this action and looked at Hugo. The dinner ended, and I went to my room to rest. I didn't want to create a scene in front of Hugo after the spectacle he put on during dinner. The next morning, I went without fail to Hugo's office, knocked on the door, but no one answered, so I entered.

Hugo was lying on his bed, completely naked. I turned to leave, but suddenly, he called out to me from the bed. "Viktor, come, don't be shy," he said. I approached him and asked him to show me the map marking the location of the relic. He refused to reveal it, saying that the price to pay was very high. I insisted, and finally, he agreed. He got out of bed, and when he turned around, he grabbed my arms and pushed me onto the bed, lying on top of me.

I felt weird at first, but then I remembered Lua and promised myself to do this for her, to save her. I swore to take revenge. When it was over, I quickly left his room and headed to Lua's parents' room. They were waiting for me along with Álvaro. We set out to retrieve the relic the next day when Hugo came running, dressed. "Good morning, everyone. Why did you leave so quickly, Viktor? I've decided to accompany you; who better to guide you than me," Hugo said.

Everyone seemed fine with it, except me, as I would have to endure him throughout the entire journey. After getting everything ready, we left the palace, but not before speaking with Marivi, who promised that upon our return, Luther would be in the parliament, resigning from his position.

The group was finally made up of Lua's parents, Álvaro, Hugo, and me. The other governors said their goodbyes, and the city gates opened for us, closing behind us as we passed through. We had a long journey ahead to the artifact, so Hugo provided each of us with a spiritual creature in this case, a hippogriff. We got on them with a little help; they were quite large for us.

The experience was very gratifying, I must admit. Feeling the wind on my face at such high speeds was fun, a part I had to thank Hugo for. We arrived at the artifact's location quite quickly, and there was no one around. We descended to the spot and dismounted with the help of Hugo. According to him, we were situated right in front of the cave where the artifact was hidden. Legend said that one loyal to their principles and with a worthy goal would be able to pass through the stone of the cave and retrieve the artifact.

Those who were not worthy would suffer a terrible death. What I least expected was for Álvaro, in a fit of egocentrism and greed, to jump onto the stone, crashing against it and falling into the abyss. I felt his loss deeply; he had been someone very special for many years, although we were not going through the best of times now. But I had to focus; the mission was clear. I thought of my goal, to save my family and free my people from the treacherous sages and Luther, of course. I jumped.

Chapter 40

"Natalia tried to go to the restroom to hide, but she was intercepted by Diego, who obviously recognized her and told her she had to accompany them to the headquarters. Natalia had no better idea than to punch Diego in the jaw, leaving him knocked out on the floor. The rest of the guards drew their weapons and prepared to fight in front of everyone. Natalia shouted at the visitors to leave, and they obeyed, running out of the restaurant without any order.

With Davyn's help, Natalia began to fight the remaining guards, who defended themselves honorably but eventually fell defeated to the ground, partly thanks to Natalia's skills from years of service in the army and Davyn's strength, which could render their opponents unconscious with a well-aimed blow. Natalia apologized to Davyn's parents for the chaos and they both ran out of the restaurant towards the hotel.

Upon arrival, they could see their friends fighting waves of dark orbs; Mafalda's animals seemed ineffective at that moment. Unexpectedly, Davyn revealed something no one expected: he was also chosen, with the power to manipulate the minds of his adversaries. Slowly, thanks to the stone walls created by Gonzalo, they managed to regroup with their friends. Luis said he didn't have enough energy yet to create a second portal.

They resisted several waves, causing everyone present to quickly tire. This time, they had no escape, and even Luther was present in the attack, leading his troops.They heard a voice calling out to them it was Laura, urging them to follow her quickly. The chosen ones obeyed and began to gradually retreat, giving Luther the impression that they were surrendering.Laura was waiting for them at a back door of the hotel, holding it open for them.

They rushed through the door, closing it behind them and quickly barricading it with various objects lying around. With Laura leading, they continued running.Laura guided them to her laboratory, re-entering through the service entrance. They ran to the weapons and armor section, where Laura provided them with the best energy weapons they had, along with advanced-level invisibility armor, completely illegal.

Berto offered Laura the opportunity to accompany them; otherwise, they would come after her for treason and arms trafficking .Laura had no choice but to accept. After all, Berto was right; they would come for her now. They left the building again and asked Luis if he had enough energy; he affirmed, so he quickly created another portal. Luis didn't know which direction to set it for, as returning to the Horseshoe Kingdom would be too dangerous, and Lukotico would likely have been moved by then.

At that moment, he remembered his past life as a Teherita navy officer but chose not to share his story with anyone, feeling regretful about that time.At that time, he had just lost his parents and was in a foster home. The house was big, and he lived with his two adoptive parents and their five black cats. Every night, they had dinner together, always arguing for any apparent reason. After dinner, it was always his turn to do the dishes while they continued arguing, sometimes even resulting in physical fights.One day he saw his mother crouched on the bathroom floor, the room completely stained in red. Luis was very scared.

Upon seeing him, his mother hurriedly closed the bathroom door.Half an hour later, his mother emerged from the bathroom, crying and totally covered in red, without looking at Luis; she went outside and yelled for the first patrol she saw. They quickly arrived at the scene, without asking what had happened; they arrested his adoptive mother. It wasn't until ten minutes later, a second patrol with a doctor arrived.They couldn't save his father; it was already too late. They took them both to the headquarters, where his mother was charged with murder, and he was cleared of all crimes.

That night, Luis slept on a bench at the headquarters, alone, with nowhere to go, no family to stay with.The next morning, officers accompanied him to the headquarters' entrance, where a family was waiting for him. What he least expected was that his nightmare was just beginning.For years, he had to endure torture from his parents, such as abuse and flagellation.His parents belonged to the Teheritas, an extremist faction of Samiz nationalism, against any being beyond the six Samiz realms.

They forced him to watch when Thomix arrived in the subterranean kingdom and was immediately beaten to death by the Teheritas; his parents participated in Thomix's beating.Luis was forced to join the Teheritas, eventually becoming an officer and carrying out missions for them, going against his principles. He moved to the Teheritas' stronghold. One day, his parents died in an attempted coup against the emperors' regime; that day, Luis finally felt free.

He decided to flee the stronghold and hide, moving to a different realm until he finally settled in the Horseshoe Kingdom with a new identity. Luis decided it was time to confront his past, and based on his knowledge of Teheritian protocols, prisoners should be confined in the stronghold until after the trial. That's where Lukotico should be; without thinking, he decided to create the portal. They began crossing the portal, slowly. They started hearing noises in the distance. They weren't concerned until they saw a light orb in one of the laboratory corridors; somehow, they had been located, or so they thought. Neither Mafalda nor Juan had time to cross the portal; they were surrounded by dark orbs led by Luther.

"Get out of wherever you are! The portal is here; at some point, you'll have to cross it," Luther shouted into the void. No one said anything; apparently, they hadn't been seen due to the invisibility suits. That was good news. The bad news was that Hector, the leader of the Teheritas, had just appeared. The scene was frightening; the orbs remained completely silent while Luther searched for the chosen ones. Somehow, Hector winked at Juan and murmured for them to leave, that he would take care of Luther.

To everyone's surprise, Hector secretly uttered words that changed Mafalda and Juan's future, allowing them to cross the portal. "Come to me Zor'gath, Nephralyx, Xul'thor, Vex'tri, lZyth'kan, Mal'drak, Zargothar, Vor'gul, Draemor, and Xer'than." Suddenly, ten demons appeared in Luther's sight, causing the dark orbs to fight against them.

This created a reliable enough distraction for Mafalda and Juan to cross the portal. After crossing the portal, they found themselves in one of the main halls of the Teherita stronghold. They all hugged without removing their invisibility suits. Berto was the first to suggest investigating the place. Everyone agreed; they needed to find Lukotico. Juan suggested going to the dungeons, but Natalia preferred to split from the rest, along with Davyn, to cover more ground.

Mafalda and Berto also decided to separate from the group. The last group consisted of Juan, Luis, and Laura. The first group, Natalia and Davyn, decided to investigate the halls, which were all empty until they reached the main dining hall located in the east wing of the stronghold. This dining hall was the largest room in the stronghold and was filled with guards peacefully dining. In the distance, an officer could be seen giving a speech. The second group, Mafalda and Berto, moved through the rooms and adjoining halls to the halls.

Everything was unprotected. They entered Hector's room; they knew it was his by an indicator sign on the door. They started rummaging through his things, curious about Hector. He had betrayed Luther and was a chosen one, so why didn't he leave with them when he had the chance? His bed was too big even for one person; perhaps he had a partner. Under the bed, they found a note, which they read:"Dear chosen ones, I am Hector, I am like you.

I apologize for not being able to help you yet; I have a very important task, and that is to finish off Luther as soon as possible. He has caused too much harm. I made a mistake when I accepted leadership in the Teheritas; I should not have allowed him to build his portal to the Antler world here. If you're reading this, I'm sorry; I will try to help you as much as I can, but Luther has control over the entire Teherita order. I don't trust anyone.The portal is in the basement, next to the supply warehouse.

Good luck; see you there.Mafalda and Berto ran towards the basement, where indeed they found the portal, a semicircular structure forged with rare metals, probably not from the Samiz realms but from the outside, likely from the lower rings, a completely unknown region to them. They had only heard legends about that place, saying that beings of other races lived there.

The point was, they had to tell the rest of the group.When they turned around, they noticed the portal starting to glow, and from it emerged a small being a small baby red dragon, but full of light. It looked at them with pleading eyes. Mafalda fell in love with it instantly and decided, without asking Berto, to adopt it. She grabbed it and put it in one of her pockets. They left the room.

They all regrouped in the same place they had separated before. Each one shared what they had found. Mafalda showed the light orb. Juan mentioned that the dungeons were empty, but he overheard some guards saying that in one of the halls, a slave auction was being prepared. At that moment, the first group confirmed what Juan said, stating that in one of the halls, full of guards, an auction was being prepared, and Lukotico was likely there.They rushed to the main hall. It was even more crowded with guards than before.

Through a small gap in the door, they could see guests arriving at the hall. They were probably mercenaries looking to recruit new members. They gradually took their seats until there was a moment of complete silence in the hall, and everyone turned toward the door where we were.They were all so focused that they didn't notice what was happening behind them. When they turned around, they saw Luther and Hector looking at them in amazement.

They tried to resist, but they were arrested by Hector's guards. They were taken behind the group, where they joined the rest of the slaves.They entered the hall, and the visitors started applauding Luther and Hector. Looking back, they could see dozens of slaves. Some were familiar faces, like Francisco and Barbara. They looked at each other with sorrow.

When they reached the hall, they climbed onto a small raised platform.From the podium, Luther delivered a welcome speech to everyone present, saying:"Distinguished guests,It is an honor and a pleasure to give you the warmest welcome to this annual and extraordinary auction. Today, we gather to celebrate the beauty of the exotic, to explore the treasures that the world offers us, and to enjoy the excitement that only an occasion like this can bring.Firstly, I want to express my sincerest gratitude to each of you for joining us in this gathering.

Your presence here is a testament to your curiosity, your passion for the exceptional, and your appreciation for the unusual. I am sure that the wonders we have on display will capture your imagination and awaken your sense of adventure.This annual auction is a meeting that transcends the boundaries of the everyday. Here, we will unleash the magic of the unknown, the charm of the unusual, and the opportunity to own something truly special.

In this auction, I encourage you to be carried away by emotion, to follow your intuition, and to participate with enthusiasm.

Remember that we are here to celebrate the beauty of diversity, the power of creativity, and the wonder of the unexplored. It is in these moments where passions are unleashed and opportunities present themselves for those willing to seize them.Finally, I wish all present a night full of excitement, discovery, and satisfaction.

May today's experience bring you new perspectives, connect your hearts with the world, and allow you to take home treasures that awaken your senses and enrich your lives.Without further ado, it is an honor to start this auction. May the bids be generous, the hearts filled with emotion, and the hands raised with determination.

Let the auction of the exotic begin!Let's go!" Luther announced .They started auctioning Francisco, followed by Barbara. The pack of both was offered at 500 sapphires and a pink emerald.Luther was pleased, selling them.At that moment, a voice interrupted the voice belonged to Viktor."

Chapter 41

"Viktor arrived at a small cave, which was filled with jewels. He was in a hurry, so he didn't take the time to look around at everything. Instead, he went straight for the staff; its handle was shaped like a parrot. He wasn't sure if that was the right staff. He left the cave and saw everyone looking at him in surprise, even Hugo.

I told them about my plan to rescue everyone, and both of them agreed. We agreed to meet at the main plaza of the dome, alongside the other people who would support us. He tasked Lua's parents with gathering everyone while he rescued his brother. Hugo promised to lead everyone to the dome where they would meet up.

I said goodbye to them, and just as Hugo had told me, I thought about my brother, how much I missed him, until I heard a voice behind me. It was his brother."

Chapter 42

Well, well, well, look what we have here! It's Luther with his little slave Hektor, having a good time selling my friends, huh? Well, I regret to inform you, Luther, that your fun's about to end. Hand over my brother and his friends, unless you want to suffer Viktor said.

But look who's here, Viktor, Lukotico's little brother! You seem new to this auction business. But if you want your brother back, you'll have to win the bid Luther asserted. That's not happening, Luther. My brother is not for sale, got it? Viktor threatened. Then you'll have to take him by force. Good luck, Viktor, Luther concluded.

At that moment, Viktor grasped his staff and recited an incantation:"In the confines of eternity, where the threads of time converge,From the stars that trace the constellation of destiny,I awaken the ancient power that lies within the depths of the cosmos.With intertwined words and resonating energy,I summon a call to the guardians of the future,Soldiers of light, warriors of tomorrow.

May your suits shine with sublime technology,Your armors gleam with unstoppable strength,Your hearts beat to the rhythm of bravery.From the realms of machines and circuits,From the farthest galaxies and unexplored worlds,Answer my call and unite in a single purpose.Let waves of energy flow through you,Infusing power into every fiber of your being,Transforming you into an unstoppable, invincible force.I conjure the legions of the future,May the wind caress your robotic wings,May the light of the stars guide your way.

Rise, army of tomorrow!Face the challenges with wisdom and courage,Protect hope, fight for a radiant future," Viktor concluded.At that moment, hundreds of orbs of light appeared, giving no time for the guards to react. Meanwhile, Hektor summoned his dozen demons. Luther managed to escape while Viktor rescued his friends.He told them they needed to return to the world of Antler; his mother and Lua were still captured.

He said if they all held hands without letting go, they could travel together, including Hektor.Viktor wished to be in the main square of the dome, and so it was. Upon opening his eyes, he found hundreds of fellow citizens carrying solidarity banners. Viktor, upon seeing this, decided it was time to put an end to the sages.He led everyone to the palace of the sages, heavily guarded. But this did not deter Viktor. Levitating a few meters above the ground, he shouted at the top of his lungs:"Attack! They won't be able to handle all of us!" Viktor yelled.

Everyone charged forward, overwhelming the sages' guards. Gonzalo smashed the door open with a powerful rock. Inside, dozens of guards stood. Davyn positioned himself in front and stunned all the guards with his power.Viktor surged forward, running into the main hall, where hundreds of guards and Sage Santhiago were still present.

Once again, he leaped from the platform, this time accompanied by his friends. As they landed, they assumed combat positions and demanded the release of Lua and her mother, but the sages adamantly refused, stating that their corpses must be cold for them to release their mother. Viktor shouted, emitting a sonic blade from his voice that cut through the air at lightning speed, slicing the throats of Santhiago and all the guards in the room.

The remaining individuals were left petrified by the scene. Quickly, they freed Lua and Viktor's mother, and as Viktor and Lua shared a passionate kiss, tears streamed down Lua's face as she silently mouthed, "Thank you." Lua collapsed to the ground. The sonic blade had struck Lua's abdomen, causing her to lose consciousness rapidly, bleeding out. Viktor began to scream, shattering all the pillars in the room.

The others fled the room as the ceiling threatened to collapse upon Viktor. Lukotico approached him, delivered a slap, and tearfully said,"Viktor, using primal powers without thinking has consequences, remember? There's no time to waste now. Come, let's go before it gets worse."As the ceiling began to crumble, the brothers rose from the ground.

Closing the door behind them, as they exited, the ceiling shattered, causing a tremendous noise and shaking throughout the building. Viktor, along with Lukotico, teleported outside the palace while Viktor continued to cry for his beloved. The rest of the group was already outside, waiting for them. Seeing Viktor in tears, his mother approached him, hugging him and thanking him for being so brave to rescue her.

She thanked everyone present for their cooperation. Viktor joined his mother in gratitude, promising that they needed to do a better job in choosing who should govern the dome and that the governor should be capable of making the Antler people prosper. Lua's parents approached Viktor and whispered that Luther had fallen into the trap set by the rulers of the Republic of Light. Laura ran up to Viktor to share her plan, which involved everyone wearing invisibility suits provided by her.

Lukotico and Viktor would distract Luther while the invisible ones surrounded him, using the chosen light to encase him. Viktor relayed the plan to the rest of the group, and no one objected. The plan seemed promising, but in practice, it might not work perfectly. However, they had to try. They couldn't let Luther roam free, not after what he had caused. They asked Luis to create the portal to the Republic of Light, but he couldn't because he had never been there. Hugo offered his hippogriffs to transport them there.

Everyone mounted the hippogriffs without assistance and bid farewell to the others who had accompanied them during the palace attack. They flew through the frigid winds until they reached the Republic of Light, where upon seeing Hugo, they were allowed to enter directly. They entered the parliament; the entrance was crowded with followers waiting to see the High Inquisitor. The group bypassed them and entered the parliament. Luther was standing on the platform, speaking. The invisible ones moved ahead of the group and surrounded Luther.

Viktor and Lukotico burst open the doors of the chamber with a loud noise, making their presence known. "Here we meet again, Luther. This time, you won't get away," Viktor promised. "I don't think you understand where you are or who you're talking to. I am Luther, the High Inquisitor of this place. Everyone you see here obeys me. You are the ones surrounded. Seize them!" Luther ordered."Luther, I, Marivi, ruler of the republic, have a question for you. Be honest.

According to one of the principles of the republic and the treaty with the Antler, it's forbidden to interact with the Samiz. Have you interacted with them? Have you enslaved their leaders to be your puppets?" Marivi asked."Filthy traitors! How could you ally yourselves with them, our most bitter archenemies, the Antler?" Luther insulted."High Inquisitor Luther,Today, we find ourselves at a moment of deep introspection and duty. It is with sorrow and determination that I address you to confront a delicate and extremely important situation.

Epilogue

The following week, elections were held within the dome to choose the representative of the Antler people. Viktor's mother also ran in the elections with the idea of building more domes, expanding, and strengthening friendship with the Republic of Light. Kerry emerged victorious with an overwhelming majority of votes, but she chose to include all the candidates in her government to have a wider range of opinions.

Viktor and Lukotico returned home and together they fed Orca, Viktor's pet. They felt a sense of peace, saddened by Lua's loss but content. Over the next few days, Viktor visited Lua's home to support her parents in overcoming the loss of their daughter. They appreciated these frequent visits.

Each of the elected representatives decided it was best to return home. They felt they had no further role in the dome, and their families must have been missing them after weeks away. Now, at least, the Samiz emperors had a bit more freedom in decision-making, which benefited the kingdoms and led them to thrive.